PROMISE TO PAY

BY

ROBERT S. LEVITZ

Inspired by an actual event

Published by Washington House
A division of Trident Media Company
801 N Pitt Street, Suite 123
Alexandria, VA 22314 USA

Dedication

To the real Henry who showed me the value of a corporate culture and to Kal who showed me the value of a family culture.

Though inspired by an actual event, any names of characters are purely fictitious. Places and locations have also been changed.

Robert S. Levitz

Bob Levitz has been part of the insurance and financial services community for over forty years. As a featured speaker, he has entertained many with his wit and insights. Recently retired as CEO of a large financial services company, he has turned to his life-long ambition of  writing. In this, his first novel, Bob has provided a glimpse into the inner workings of a major American corporation, a large mutual life insurance company. He has brought to bear his knowledge of sales and people and exposes his personal preference for those gentler corporate days.

Residing in Deerfield, Illinois, on Chicago's North Shore, Bob also provides a look at Chicago behind the scenes and his love of the city shines through. With a wife, three sons and eight grandchildren, it may be difficult for the reader to envision this grandfather writing what is, in part, an exciting, but also erotic first novel.

PROLOGUE

He had spent the last two days bargaining and pleading hoping to persuade. He had been invited to appear in front of a congressional committee investigating charges by his industry that its companies were being unfairly taxed. His feeling, as he sat in his first class seat on a United flight out of Washington, D.C., was that in the end it was all a charade—congressmen and women whose minds were made up, creating the fiction that they were open-minded listeners.

Truth be known, as his flight headed to Chicago and home, the disappointment of the brick wall he and his compatriots had hit was momentarily forgotten. Instead, he sank back in his aisle seat, diet Coke in hand, and as his plane soared thirty thousand feet into the sky his thoughts were centered on Friday morning, tomorrow.

In the beginning there was a slight hoarseness and he really hadn't paid much attention to it. At his age, small aches, pains, and other slight maladies were somewhat routine. Then came the constant heartburn and the unpleasant burping. Better cut back on the coffee, he had thought. After explaining his symptoms to Dr. Weinstein during a routine physical the good doctor had said little, but ordered a variety of tests.

When morning arrived, though he was, by nature, not a nervous person, the starkness of the room, the whiteness of it, and the large machine sitting in the center of it was, even to him, unsettling. The thought that his body would be entering the center of the machine's universe for scoping and that the technicians, physicians, and others would see him totally exposed, to the very core of his being, really unnerved him. As his body slid inside the machine and music drifted to his brain through earphones, he did not feel in any way soothed. As the MRI machine droned on with its muted anvil-like pounding he became convinced that, whatever the test revealed, it would be catastrophic. His physician's obvious alarm and concern over his symptoms somehow peaked his intuition and instinctively he knew that he had reached the near end of his sixty-eight-year-old life.

As the patriarch of his family, whom he dearly loved, and the leader of a major American company, he knew, deep down, two terrible secrets. The first of these was that he was somehow certain he was dying. The second of the secrets was that neither he, which was to be expected, nor his company, which would be unexpected by many, was ready for this event.

His personal affairs were very much in order, but his business affairs were another story entirely. Although the company was sound and safe as long as he was there to run it, his single failing as its leader was that he had not developed a workable plan of succession. Were he to die, chaos could result and many innocent people would be hurt. The thought was less then comforting.

The test droned on until the machine's final moan and groan when, at long last, it shut down.

PART I
APRIL – AUGUST 1996

CHAPTER 1

The mid-April sunlight reflected from the windows of the Insurance Company of America building. Eighty stories tall, sleek and contemporary, it rose imposingly above the Chicago skyline. The building occupied an entire square block and was located between Erie and Ontario Streets on Michigan Avenue. One could enter from Michigan Avenue on the east or Chicago's famous Rush Street on the west side. Opened in 1989, ICA occupied the top thirty floors. Offices and retail accounted for the rest of the space.

At the very top of the building, on the eightieth floor, WICA-FM played light classical music and passed out traffic information to its listeners. The view from the eightieth was awesome. On a clear day one could see as far north as the Baha'i Temple in Wilmette. To the south smoke from the steel mills of Gary, Indiana, rose into the cloudless sky. One floor below, ICA had located its executive offices. When visitors stepped off the elevator they were greeted by a warm, business-like environment that, through the use of beautiful woods and artwork, conveyed a feeling of financial strength, but was not at all austere or aristocratic. The elevators opened into a circular corridor and a sign pointed to the right for those interested in visiting the company's legal department.

Another sign pointing left, said simply: Executive Offices and Board Room, and led to a seating area with a receptionist. Nancy Wagner, a matronly looking woman in her late forties, sat outside of a tall, walnut-paneled door that led to president and chairman of the board, Henry Rothblatt's office.

By education an actuary, Henry Rothblatt, born in Toronto, Canada, after graduating from college, had taken a position with ICA over forty-five years ago. Henry was a spry sixty-eight year old with the keenest of minds. He was lean and wiry and always seemed to have a bemused look on his face; a face which was at once very expressive yet difficult to read.

When Henry had been appointed to the presidency of ICA twenty years earlier, later assuming the position of chairman of the board, the company was just emerging as a life insurance company powerhouse.

Under Rothblatt's skillful and tight-fisted rein, the company had blossomed, and today it was one of the largest mutual life insurance companies in the country.

Most lay people did not know that fundamentally, there are two types of life insurance companies, mutual and stock. A mutual company is owned by its policyholders. Each one owns a fractional share of the company, similar to a stockholder in a public corporation. As a group they theoretically have input into the direction of their company and share, through dividends, in company profits.

Alternatively, a stock life insurance company is owned by stock-holders. It wouldn't be far-fetched to say that while a mutual company is operated for the benefit of the policyholders, a stock company operates for the benefit of its stockholders. Policyholders of a stock company are not necessarily short-changed, but on a crucial issue, the interests of the stockholder and the policyholder may be in conflict, and the stockholder is generally going to win.

Henry had a grim look on his face as he walked off the elevator, past Nancy, and entered his office. The look was unrelenting and Henry did not utter his daily, "Good morning, Nancy." Nancy thought he appeared unsettled as she set his morning mail before him, and she looked closely at her boss of the last twenty years. She had become his secretary at about the same time he had assumed his office as president of ICA. She had answered his phone, sorted his mail, scheduled appointments, and screened those looking for his most valuable time. Nancy Wagner knew Henry Rothblatt better than anyone in the world except Ruth, Henry's wife.

When Nancy returned to Henry's desk after fetching his first cup of morning coffee from a pot located in a small alcove between his office and the boardroom, she set it before him and looked at him quizzically, "Bad night?"

"No, no," Henry responded. "Do I look as though I had a bad night?"

"Well, I'd say you look both preoccupied and tired."

"You worry too much; I'm just fine."

As she started to step back toward her desk, she heard him say, "Thanks, thanks Nancy, for everything." She thought once again how very odd he was acting this morning.

CHAPTER 2

Several floors below Henry's office was the Agency Department. Any other business would have referred to it as the Sales or perhaps Marketing Department. It was where the company's people dreamed up all sorts of ideas to market its products. This was where the sales goals were set and hopefully met. Everyone understood that until someone sold something nothing happened. Field sales managers, known as general agents or GA's, were interviewed and recruited here. The GA's were charged with the responsibility of recruiting and training new agents, and building their local sales organizations. Each GA was an entrepreneur, an independent business person.

The Agency Department was run by David Rourke, and his was an important and critical role. After starting as an agent, David became a GA for ICA. At thirty-seven years of age, David had been with the company in his present capacity for over seven years and he had made his presence felt through shrewd management of a department that had been small and in disarray before his arrival. He was responsible for establishing many new agencies throughout the country and strengthening existing relationships. The field loved David and felt he was a strong and loyal leader, very much one of them.

David had made it clear from the outset that he understood the value of the company's agents and general agents. The GA's, realizing that David had come from their ranks, adopted a somewhat provincial attitude toward him. Management aspirants from other companies began to realize that ICA had a winner in David Rourke and they wanted to join the fun. Capitalizing on David's popularity, ICA began to recruit the best young field management people in the country. For the past several years, David had ICA on a roll and picking up speed.

There are two types of field management systems in the life insurance industry. A manager is usually an employee and, as such, subject to the whims of an employer. If a company tells a manager he is going to change agencies and locations, the manager goes. If he or she refuses it could effectively end their career with that company.

3

On the other hand, the general agent is an independent contractor, he or she pays the rent and other overhead. In a management system, the manager accepts little of the financial risk and is usually on a salary plus incentive; for the general agent there is no salary. The GA, however, earns a higher emolument of commission on each unit of business than a manager. If he is a good business person and keeps his overhead in line, the GA will do well financially, because he is a true entrepreneur accepting all the risks of running his own show. Subsequently, he reaps the appropriate award including ownership of his business.

David Rourke and Henry Rothblatt both understood the fundamental difference between manager and GA and they built a sales organization on that difference. Recruiting new GA's was no problem once exposed to the system and the culture of partnership, field, and company. They were also exposed to the partnership which extended to ICA's policyholder owners. A GA candidate was hooked when he realized the culture was a reality. David had learned well serving at Henry Rothblatt's feet. They both believed in ICA and all it stood for, and their enthusiasm was contagious. Employees and field people alike became locked into the partnership for all the right reasons.

CHAPTER 3

From childhood David had been blessed with great interpersonal skills, and he interacted with people in an extraordinary manner. His personality was like a magnet drawing people to him. One would have been hard pressed to find an enemy of David's, whether business or personal. His ethics and integrity were unquestioned. Growing up in a middle-class neighborhood of St. Paul, Minnesota, David benefited from his neighborhood and school relationships by absorbing the tough, humorous, and intense heritage of his Irish ancestry, while his Scandinavian friends and schoolmates gave him great insight into their wonderful system of family values and gentleness. His parents, both feisty Irish, took him as a child to visit Ireland and their family. He cherished memories of those trips to the "old Sod." In recent years David had been mentored by Henry Rothblatt who guided and showed him how to blend his compassion and empathy with the tough-mindedness that was necessary to be successful in a corporate career, and he prided himself on being able to make the tough decisions. David did not mind in the least admitting that he was Henry's protegé.

David loved his career and he felt he owed a great deal to Henry. There was not only a mutual respect between the two, but a genuine fondness despite the age difference. They met frequently outside the office, played golf together and occasionally tennis. They also lunched together frequently, and David delighted in the way he was able to amuse Henry with his innate ability to tell jokes and stories. David had a knack with accents and Henry belly-laughed whenever David used them in telling one of his preposterous tales. For his part, Henry loved to listen to David but would never be caught himself telling a joke.

Every Monday morning at six A.M. they would meet at the East Bank Club, work out, and then from seven-thirty to nine o'clock they would have a business breakfast. This Monday was no different, and after their workout, shower, and shave, David walked toward the same table he and Henry almost always shared.

The surroundings at the East Bank Club were wonderful. It was a contemporary, self-contained shrine to slim, starving, sleek-looking, carrot juice- drinking women and men to whom sweat was a badge of honor. Charged with energy it was a gathering place for Chicago's movers and shakers, its young and its beautiful. It was also a well-known meeting place for singles. David was single but never seriously looked at the health club as a place to meet women, not that the handsome young man with the dark hair tinged with gray was above looking at a good-looking young lady. Quite the contrary, as serious-minded as David was about business, he was somewhat cavalier about his personal life. It was a bone of contention with his mentor.

"Good morning, David." Henry, unlike David, was not a sharp dresser. His suits, though custom made, lacked the sharpness of David's own attire. On this morning, Henry wore a tired shade of brown in a two-button suit under which he had on a pale blue shirt and an expensive, but nondescript, tie.

"Good morning to you," David said, flashing a smile which Henry always thought warm and charming.

Henry eyed David and remarked, "Nice get-up; I suppose I just never developed the flair you have for clothes." Henry observed the good-looking, square-jawed youngster before him dressed in a tailored navy blue suit with a bright tie of navy, gray, and yellow and a yellow pocket handkerchief flashing from the jacket pocket. Spotting the tie, Henry said, "Someday, when I can afford it, I'm going to get me one of those."

The two men had talked many times about personal finance. David was cavalier about money; Henry completely the opposite. But why not, thought Henry, he's single and earns a handsome salary. David's bonus this year would be more than Henry had made in total just fifteen years ago.

A pretty young waitress set orange juice and coffee before them, having served them both breakfast on many occasions. She also set down a basket of miniature muffins and fresh-baked bagels, and as Henry knifed a small amount of cream cheese onto an egg bagel, he looked up at David. "We need to talk," Henry said, quite seriously.

David saw the serious look on Henry's face and took a sip of

6

coffee. Setting the cup down, he backed up his chair, crossed his legs, and asked that Henry continue.

Ever direct, Henry paused only momentarily and then: "I'm dying, David, and this causes two very serious problems. The first is, of course, the obvious. You know how much the family means to me; I love them all dearly. I do know that Ruth will get through this, however, and she'll have the family for her support system." Before Henry could continue, David tried to interrupt. This was absurd, he thought, and the runaway train wasn't slowing down. When Henry looked up and saw his good friend about to lose it, he continued in order to help David regain his composure. "The second problem is also serious, perhaps even catastrophic in nature. I'm going to require your assistance."

"Anything," the younger man managed to get out.

"David, you and I know that my great failing as ICA's leader has been my inability to create future leadership for the company. God knows I've tried. At one time I thought it might be you; but you indicated you felt incapable and I understood. You're a great leader of men but without the financial abilities that also are needed. On the other hand, we have a number of financially capable individuals but without your ability to capture the troops."

"Henry"— David still was trying to make sense of what he was hearing. He was upset and shaking with rage at any disease that might take his leader, mentor, and friend from him. "Henry, what the hell are you talking about? Are you crazy? You're not going anywhere; it's a matter of the right doctors. What exactly is the problem? What have you got? Whom have you seen?"

The lean, good-looking, older man sat back in his chair and exhaled. "Cancer. Advanced esophageal cancer. It's almost always fatal and, unfortunately, quite fast moving. I'm being attended to medically; but I desperately need your help working out details of a transition."

"You know I'll do anything for you and ICA, but can't we discuss your course of action concerning your illness?"

"No," was Henry's terse reply. "David, I don't have a lot time and we need to develop a succession strategy. Can I count on you?"

7

In a nano second the years flashed in front of David. The years of being the student to wise old professor Rothblatt. The classes in ethics, morality and the attention to the building, maintenance, and nurturing of a wonderful and benevolent corporate culture.

David pushed away from the table and stood. There, in the middle of the East Bank Club restaurant, in front of all the other people sitting around them, David, with tears in his eyes, leaned over and hugged, then kissed Henry Rothblatt on the cheek. He placed his hand on top of Henry's which were folded on the table in front of him and whispered, "I love you, boss. You can count on me, but I need twenty-four hours." David abruptly turned and walked away to collect himself. Henry, watching his protégé, understood and knew he truly could count on David.

CHAPTER 4

Whatever David's income, and no matter how he spent it, no one would ever accuse him of squandering it on his living quarters. Located in Wrigleyville, a unique Chicago neighborhood near Wrigley Field, home of the Cubs baseball team, his apartment was on the first floor of a typical Chicago two-flat. Each floor of the building consisted of one apartment. The second floor was occupied by three young men only a couple of years out of college. David's apartment was decorated in early bachelor, and then in poor taste. The color black was everywhere. The place looked like Hugh Hefner's early Playboy pad—lap tables, sofas, chairs, even bed linens were all black, broken only by an occasional and poorly placed splash of red or white. All the pieces of furniture were present, but not necessarily in the right places.

After climbing the steps from the street and turning the ornate gold handle on the front door of the building, he entered the foyer and checked for mail. Once in his apartment he tossed the mail onto the kitchen table without so much as a look. Opening the fridge, he pulled out a Heineken or Heini, as he liked to call it, and moved into a room he called his den. The room had a small desk where he kept his personal papers. A comfortable square leather chair and ottoman faced the TV. David, tired and disheveled, removed his suit jacket, sat in the chair, and let himself sink deeply into it. His black and red suspenders fit right in with the decor of the room. He was exhausted, emotionally and physically. As he sat, his hand holding the beer out to the side, he placed his feet on the ottoman. He looked drained, the whites of his blue eyes were red and he was concentrating deeply.

His mind had a unique ability to compartmentalize. Henry's imminent death was in one of those compartments, at least for the moment. For now all of his thoughts were focused on a possible replacement for the man he knew to be an extraordinary chief executive. He had thought about little all day but Henry and the succession issue. There were, he thought, possible candidates. Some of them David thought of as okay, but none did he see as outstanding.

He kept turning over in his mind the qualities he felt it would take. Henry, he knew, was an actuary by education and early practice, but Henry was also a great salesman and, as with most great salesmen, you never realized you were being sold. Henry was also a wonderfully and totally compassionate man, but he could make tough decisions. He was an incisive thinker who would readily accept feedback. The man could be a charmer but also as persuasive as hell. His heart was as big as a lion and he had wonderful people skills. He was sharp and sensitive, able to size up situations and people almost instantly. Henry was a leader who captured loyalty from others by offering his in return. But most of all, David mused to himself, for an actuary, he was a great salesman.

Henry had sold David quite a few years ago. Henry had persuaded David, a young and successful general agent, to renounce his independence and instead work for ICA to develop a first class sales force. At the time David was footloose and fancy free. At the firm he ran his own show and, by exhibiting many of the very qualities he attributed to Henry, he had built a fine sales organization in St. Paul and was doing very well for himself. Henry had sold David on the higher purpose of building ICA into what would become a company known for commitment to its community and one that cared deeply about its employees and associates in the field. Most importantly, it would be known for the fairness with which it treated its constituency, its policyholders. They would build a company that, as Henry put it, "does what is right."

It appealed to David, and he bought into the dream through Henry's magnetic charisma. He was never sorry. Henry mentored him and David knew he was better for the experience. He had learned to give of himself, to the city, friends, and business associates. Now, seven years after joining ICA's management team, David felt good about himself. More importantly, through his association with Henry Rothblatt, he felt very proud of what they were accomplishing.

David found it difficult to think about possible candidates to succeed Henry. He had no idea whom Henry might select to be his successor in the ICA boardroom, but his intuition, which he trusted, told him that this would not be an easy decision.

CHAPTER 5

At home, after a few hours at the office, Henry shared his day with Ruth. He spoke of his meeting with David that morning and, to his longtime bride, described David's reaction.

"Well, you can hardly blame the young man. My God, Henry, he worships you. So many people do, you know, darling." That kind of talk made him feel uncomfortable so he started in another direction.

"Ruth, I'm thinking of asking Dick Washington to act as interim president and vice-chairman of the board during my recovery. We've agreed that if I want the best chance for remission, we'll have to be aggressive. That means large doses of chemotherapy and radiation which will knock me on my fanny. I'm likely to be out awhile. I need someone capable of keeping things together until I can return. What do you think?"

Ruth Rothblatt, Henry's wife of over forty years, was an imposing looking woman. Fastidious in her neatness, she was dressed plainly. But, like her husband, she commanded respect by her very demeanor. The past week, ever since she and Henry talked with Dr. Weinstein at his office, had been difficult for her. She had heard Dr. Weinstein describe the cancer afflicting the man she loved, and she had heard his prognosis as well.

"Henry has about a 10 percent chance of surviving for two years. With aggressive treatment we might get those numbers to 50 percent for five years. You must understand that aggressive means just that. Many patients find it totally overwhelming. We just don't know exactly how any single patient will react," Dr. Weinstein had told them. There had been no doubt in either of their minds that Henry would elect the aggressive treatment.

"Well, I don't really know, dear. I always thought you had some reservations about Dick. You never seemed quite comfortable about him."

"I suppose there is some truth to that, but he has the knowledge it would take and my concerns about him are of a more personal nature."

"Are you talking about that incident at the club? Honestly, you men and your golf. As I think about it, Dick seems a logical choice,

11

dear, you hand-picked him for the board, and he's a friend. But, what about his present position?"

"He retired about a month ago. He's available, particularly on a temporary basis. I admit to some concerns, but time is of the essence here and Dick does have the longevity on our board and a fair insight about our business. Think I'll set up a meeting with him."

CHAPTER 6

Many still think of Chicago as a steak and beef town. Long after the death of the Chicago stockyards visitors still come to town expecting a large juicy steak, and good steak houses are plentiful. Gibson's on Rush Street was a particular favorite. But this night they felt like Italian, and what all those visitors didn't realize was that Chicago abounds with some of the best Italian eateries in the country. Right near the top of the list was the Rosebud Café on Taylor Street in Little Italy.

Chicago may be the most ethnic city in America. Its neighborhoods are sprawling and diverse. In each ethnic neighborhood, from Greek to Chinese, from Italian to Jewish, restaurants serve some of the best and most authentic food. Taylor Street was in the center of Chicago's Italian neighborhood and everyone from Mayor Daley to the governor came to Taylor Street for an Italian meal from one the street's many great eating establishments. Rosebud was the acknowledged king with an atmosphere that was all at once romantic, scuzzy, neapolitan, and intriguing. Famous for their Chicken Vesuvio Supreme, made with their homemade spicy sausage, many a crooked nose had enjoyed a meal and cigar at Rosebud.

As they left the restaurant and the doorman brought around his red S500 Mercedes convertible, Dick felt full from the pasta and sausage as well as the beer and chianti. Pulling away from the curb he reached for Dena's hand and placed it over his crotch. She pulled it back and told him to behave himself, but she laughed to let him know it wasn't so terrible and also to hint at what might be yet to come.

With the top down Richard Washington headed toward the city just a few minutes away by expressway. It was a clear night, the stars were out, and it was warm, unusually warm for the late spring, and tomorrow the prediction was for a major heat wave to hit the city. At his side was a smart-looking woman in her mid-forties with short blond hair blown by the wind; she was wearing a tight, short, but expensive beige dress. She too was one of Chicago's movers and shakers.

Dena Callahan was beautiful but also accomplished. She had been recently promoted to Dean of the Business School at the

University of Chicago. Her date, Dick Washington, was handsome, gray-haired, and slightly overweight. No wonder, she thought, he liked his booze. He had a line of b.s. that kept her laughing. They met at her first board meeting. She had been asked by Henry Rothblatt of ICA to replace a woman who had moved to Europe. It was her first appointment to a major company's board. Subsequently, several other companies discovered Dena and she now sat on the board of no less than four major Chicago corporations. She had met Rothblatt at a holiday party Henry and Ruth had given the year before her appointment. Invited by friends to the party, they met at the exact time Henry had been thinking about a politically correct appointment to replace the one woman who had been on the board. He needed someone who could contribute, and the brilliant Ms. Callahan easily filled the bill.

Dena had found Dick to be handsome and attentive. She also sensed his ruthlessness which she greatly admired, and she found his cool demeanor a turn-on. Eventually they began to see one another and this led to their present affair. Fiftyish and the former president of Batem Communications, a very large manufacturer of tele-electronics equipment, she knew only that Washington had retired. It struck her as odd that anyone would retire from such a prestigious position at such an early age. She had dated married men on a couple of occasions before and really had no compunctions about the morality of it all. Dena had been married herself, but only briefly. It was a foolish marriage on her part and had taken place while she was still in college. She had found herself far too ambitious for her mate. With no particular rush to jump into another marriage, she liked her independence and the fact that she was responsible to no one except herself.

She had been raised by a doting, but very busy, small politician father who found it easier to give in to her whims than not. She found it easy to take.

Just north of the Loop and a few blocks from Rush and Division Streets the neighborhood took on a distinctly affluent look. Anchored by the Ambassador Hotel on the corner of State and Goethe, the two-story brownstones reeked of wealth and opulence. Richard's home could be nowhere else. He was city; he was glitz and show. He had the money, power, and prestige, so why not? These homes, expensive as they were, did not have garages or, if they did, they were found in a rear alley. Richard was not an alley person. He guided the convertible into a public garage about a block from his home. Usually one of the valet-parkers on duty would chauffeur him to his front door. Tonight he had Dena with him and he thought the short walk back to his place would be nice. The car was really too small for three people anyway.

He wasn't in the least worried about being seen with a woman other than his wife. This was not the kind of area where cne knew his neighbors, and Felicia, his wife of twenty-five years, was at their place in Naples, Florida. Anyway, even if Felicia had been at home, she would not have cared in the least. Theirs was a marriage of convenience, Dick Washington thought to himself—his convenience.

CHAPTER 7

On Monday morning Henry skipped his workout at the East Bank, and his usual meeting with David. The chemotherapy treatments wouldn't start until Wednesday, but his strength just wasn't there, and he knew the effects of the illness had begun to accelerate. Willing himself to dress, he took the company car to the office where he had scheduled a 10:30 A.M. meeting with his executive committee.

As he sat in a leather recliner in the alcove that separated his office from the board room, he looked about at a lifetime of family and business-related photographs hanging on the wall. His children's photographs were prominent. His daughter Jennifer was in Israel on a Kibbutz; another daughter, Jacqueline, and a son, Harold, were married, and he expected to hear any day that he would be a grandfather from one or the other. He hoped he would still be around for the event. He desperately wanted to hold his first grandchild.

On the wall to the left, Henry browsed through more than one hundred photos of himself and many others, all of whom he loved or had a genuine fondness for. The pictures had been taken at a variety of business functions, conventions, and meetings. Those were times Henry loved. He was brilliant at making everyone feel comfortable around him and that made people want to be with him. If Ruth accompanied him, he would fit in a round of golf with associates and then dine with her and those he had played with and their wives. When he was unaccompanied by Ruth, there was usually a poker game in his suite at night. To be invited to play golf with Henry Rothblatt was an honor and an event worthy of bragging about. Henry played golf or cards only with those he knew well and they in turn knew the rules: no business was ever discussed unless he brought it up and that seldom happened.

As he sipped his coffee, he began to formulate how he would disclose the events of the last week or so to his executive committee. Details would include his meeting with Richard Washington. That meeting, he felt, had gone well. Richard, of course, registered great dismay over Henry's illness, and since he had both the time and

16

know-how he quickly agreed to act as vice chair until Henry could resume his full activities, assuming he could. Dick was a board member of nearly ten years, and before he had moved into the city, he been a neighbor, which is how he and Henry originally met. Henry could not look or be more Jewish. Dick was the prototypical WASP, yet while not close, they seemed to understand one another. Both belonged to Highland Park Country Club, a decidedly nonsectarian club. They loved golf but played poorly, so they often played in foursomes together as the high handicap players. As such, they were frequently pitted against one another. Over the years they shared some laughs and developed a mutual respect for the others' competitive nature. They were both intense about business matters and each was private in nature.

His thought processes were interrupted by Nancy. "Would you like more coffee?" She stood next to his chair with pot in hand ready to pour. Henry looked up and smiled gently, but with a slight wave of his hand let her know he was finished. She took his cup without a word being spoken as Henry struggled out of his chair. Obviously the man had a physical problem; she wanted to ask about it, but didn't dare. Her heart broke and tears nearly came as she watched his weakened body search for stability. At !ast out of his chair, he walked slowly toward his desk without looking at her.

With his back to her, he said "Nancy, I'd like you to attend the executive committee meeting today."

At first she thought he might want her to take notes. She had done that on a few occasions, but as Nancy started in the direction of her desk, it suddenly came to her. My God, she thought to herself, and her knees buckled. My God, he's dying. Oh, Lord! Once the wave of nausea had passed, her next thought was that she would have to be strong, let no one interfere with whatever the boss wanted. She looked at her desk clock, it was 10:15; she had just fifteen minutes to set up Henry's office for the meeting. They never used the boardroom because Henry preferred it be used for board meetings only. On occasion, if there were too many for his office, he would relent, but not often. She placed chairs in front of Henry's desk—there would be six plus himself. When Nancy looked up, she noted

17

Henry behind his desk furiously writing notes. What a wonderful man, she thought, once again. She had everything she could do to keep from breaking apart. I'd kill for that man, she thought. He was a kind and gentle person who had over the years been a friend and father figure to her. She hoped she was wrong about him being ill, but she knew she was dead on.

CHAPTER 8

At 10:30 the executive committee gathered. David was present as head of the sales division, as was Tim Walker, the head bean counter, as David liked to refer to him. Walker was head of the actuarial department. He was a trim and proper man, small in stature, large in brains, a good man; Tim Walker was someone David respected. His department had greater responsibilities than those which immediately met the eye. Pricing the product was detailed and exacting work.

Actuaries had been described as people who looked out the back window of the car because where they had been was far more important than where they were going. Everything an actuary did was based on a perspective of history. They dealt in mortality and morbidity, how long people would live and how frequently they might become disabled. In order to construct an appropriate and profitable rate that was competitive in the marketplace, they had to consider a wide spectrum of statistics and special interests. Commission rates for sales people could not be determined without actuarial input, therefore David and Tim had a close working relationship. Tim never made a recommendation he could not back up statistically.

Daryl Green ran the company's administrative side. Intimate with computers, David seldom took issue with Daryl. He was just too knowledgeable about what was and wasn't possible administratively.

Joe Swallow, Vice President of Investments, was on hand. He was a quiet, thoughtful man.

Bob Wellington was the real power in the room, next to Henry, of course, thought David. Bob was and had been for over twenty years corporate counsel for ICA. He was a board member and a valued Rothblatt confidant.

At 10:30 exactly, Jerry Barton walked into the office of the President and Chairman of the Board Henry Rothblatt. Jerry was not high on David's list of people to have dinner with. Barton was a pompous ass, as far as David was concerned. He ran the company's group sales division and did for the mass-marketing side of the company what David did for the individual sales division. There were constant turf issues and they were frequently at each other's throats. As Barton sat down, Henry wasted no time in getting to the task at hand.

"Gentlemen," Henry began, "I'm going to set aside our usual agenda for this morning's meeting in order to speak with you about a most serious problem. The situation I speak of could become cataclysmic if it's not resolved quickly and efficiently." No one other than David knew what was coming, but their curiosity was certainly aroused. Each man, even David, edged forward as though this would allow them to hear better. At least one of the men was thinking that whatever this cataclysmic event might be it surely involved him. That was Daryl Green's nature. Henry continued: "I've been advised that I'm going to require medical treatment which will likely be very debilitating. During this period of time which, by the way, is largely unknown, I've requested that Richard Washington act as vice chairman of our board of directors and also as interim president. You all know Richard, and you will each temporarily report to him and, I trust, give him your full cooperation. He's a very successful individual, and a person I trust implicitly to help me run this company for the duration.

"I will continue on, at least for now, with the title of President and Vice Chairman. I'm not sure exactly how much I'll actually be able to contribute. Now for the real problem." Real problem, each of them wondered. Isn't this the real problem; isn't Henry Rothblatt the cataclysmic event?

"Should I not recover"... there were perfunctory interruptions from the group, each offering assurances that Henry would be fine. David sat back and wondered how specific Henry would get. He was a very private man on matters such as this. "Should I not recover," Henry repeated, "you will be forced to deal with the issue of succession."

To their credit not one man in the room thought in terms of himself at that moment. Well, David wasn't quite certain about Jerry Barton. Very quickly each man sized up the people around him in a casual way. Each was looking for the possible successor to Henry

Rothblatt, should it become necessary.

" Henry," it was chief legal counsel Bob Wellington speaking, "you've hit us with quite a load. Still I'm certain I speak for all of us on a couple of issues. First, you must know that you have each of our pledges to do whatever you and ICA may call upon us to do. However, we would appreciate it, if you feel you can share with us the specifics of your illness."

Henry turned in his chair to face away from the group sitting in front of his desk. A murky reflection of his face could be seen in the glass covering a painting over the credenza behind his desk. David noticed the painting was uncharacteristically modern. Funny, he had never paid attention to it before. The modernistic painting, he thought, showed the breadth of Henry's thinking. He was not a man that was easily pigeonholed with a description. Liberal, conservative, soft touch, tough, it depended on the situation.

After a brief pause, during which Henry was mulling over his answer, the now weary man at center stage began a brief but full explanation of his prognosis and treatment. When he had finished, the room was silent; he had pulled no punches. All needed to understand the seriousness of the situation.

"I'll set up a meeting with each of you individually on Friday. Nancy, will you take care of that? Until then please think about who you feel could permanently run this company in the event of," he paused, "my death. Who will best retain the ICA culture and give all of you the best opportunity for success at every level. I must say that I prefer choosing someone within the company if at all possible."

With that, Henry stood but asked David and Tim Walker to remain. The meeting was adjourned. David and Tim did not speak a word to each other as Henry showed the others out of his office. Though David and Tim had very different personalities they liked each other. They didn't see each other socially but they had worked well together on any number of ICA projects. David was always pushing toward an adequate level of compensation for his sales force as well as the bells and whistles that would make ICA's products more valuable and saleable. Tim, on the other hand, was always looking to balance things, in order to create profits for ICA and its policyholders and owners which were really one and the same. When Tim was right, dividends would result and the products became more competitive. David, during his tenure, had not been aware of any major mistakes on Tim's part. Add that to the respect Tim showed the sales division of the company, and David would have probably suggested Tim for the position under discussion.

Henry interrupted David's thinking when he addressed them both. "The two of you will, in one way or another, be instrumental in ICA's future; therefore I want to keep you abreast of my thinking." Henry walked back around his desk and sat. David and Tim watched him closely. His usually tanned face was pasty and it was evident he was worn out from his short morning's activities.

"Tim, you clearly would be my first choice; I believe you to possess more than adequate knowledge of our business and culture. You're fifty-two, and you and your wife have given twenty plus years to the organization. You have the confidence of our field and home office associates; your ability to solve complex problems is outstanding, and..." As Henry continued praising him, suddenly it became clear to David; Henry was not going to offer Tim the job.

"Tim, you have all the qualities I would look for in a president and CEO for this company but," Henry's voice lowered and David thought he heard a slight waver, "I cannot in good conscience recommend you to the board. Five years ago you had a serious heart attack. Fortunately, you've made a wonderful recovery and, as far as I know, you're fit and feeling well, but I cannot recommend you. The board simply wouldn't buy it. It would think it not prudent. I can only hope you understand."

Tim did not speak. He would later realize that Henry Rothblatt, in spite of all the well-intended and sincere rhetoric, had effectively ended any meaningful career for him with ICA. He could, and probably would stay on, but he would be able to coast until his retirement. Like the military, once passed over, the career is effectively ended. These facts, along with the possible loss in the near future of Henry, left Tim dazed. He said nothing; he could not think of anything worthwhile.

David finally broke the awkward silence. "Henry, if not Tim, then who? It's not a great secret that we're thin on presidential talent around here."

For the first time this morning David thought he saw a slight smile cross the boss' lips. "Thin on presidential talent, are we?" Henry sighed. "True, and I'm afraid the present president is a bit thin on ideas and energy. It's been a trying morning. Would you both excuse me? I'd like to catch a little nap before Dick arrives at one o'clock."

"Washington is coming here? Are you ready to make announcements already?" David was caught by surprise. He wasn't certain why; he knew action was needed to provide the company with the leadership it required as quickly as possible, even for the short run.

"No, no announcement yet. We're just going to have a chat and discuss a few things. We'll make an announcement in a day or two. While Dick is here I want to meet jointly with Boris and his PR people. We've got to do everything possible to retain the confidence of all of our constituencies, employees, policyholders, and, of course, the field force. I'll meet with the two of you tomorrow, but think hard for me, will you? We need someone permanent."

CHAPTER 9

When Mike Spellari's phone rang, he laid aside the papers he was looking at and picked up the receiver. After a brief and perfunctory greeting, he listened. After awhile Mike was listening hard, very hard. His face was grim and tight-lipped. His left hand was clenched in a fist and his right nearly crushed the phone's receiver. After several minutes and a short goodbye, Mike replaced the phone's handset in its cradle. He leaned back in his large black leather executive chair and closed his eyes as he processed what he had just learned.

There wasn't a tougher kid to come out of south Philly than Mike Spellari, but he was street smart, too. As a child he had a wonderful family for support, but they didn't have the money for his education so he had worked hard to put himself through college. He was a voracious reader and knew a little or a lot about almost everything. He certainly knew everything about finance and building a sales organization.

His wife and children were of paramount importance to him. They had seen his quick temper, and they lived with his combative style, but he showed them nothing but love. He was a rock and held their admiration for being a self-made man, but they also loved him for his extreme caring. He was a fountain of ideas with extraordinary charm, but still he was this tough kid from Philly. Now, sitting there in his office, he cried. He cried as though he had lost a father; he cried because he felt he was about to.

David had thought twice before calling Mike, but in the end felt he had made the right decision. He and Mike were very close. ICA's leading field manager with an extraordinary record of sales, Mike was an accomplished leader, and David and he often consulted on matters that would affect the ICA sales force. Mike was a brilliant strategist and balanced David's impulsiveness and emotionalism. Both men had Henry Rothblatt as their mentor and very close personal friend. The triangle of their relationship transcended anything described in books or classes on management.

When it came to the sales arena, Henry would lay out the

24

problem to Mike and they would jointly work toward finding a solution. David sold the solution to the field. Each did an extraordinary job with his piece of the puzzle.

Once, when Henry had decided on a course of action that was contradictory to what the rest of the life insurance industry was doing, but which was in the interest of ICA's policyholders, he knew he would need Mike's support. Like David, having grown up, from a business perspective, at Henry's feet, Mike immediately fell in line with the plan. David had asked Mike why he had accepted Henry's proposition so easily. He pointed out that while it would benefit the policyholders and to some degree also ICA, it was clearly detrimental to the sales force. Mike simply smiled and asked David a question. "Is it the right thing to do?" David, being a great salesman himself, was easily sold, and felt his respect for Mike climb to an all time high.

David was now keeping Mike involved, but a question Mike had asked when David told him about Dick Washington becoming vice chairman and acting president disturbed him. "Why that guy?" David had no good answer and responded only that "Henry sees him as a friend and qualified, I guess."

After Mike had finally composed himself he began doing what he did best. He liked to take a situation or problem and play out all of the possible scenarios and their outcomes in his mind. At that moment he was contemplating the pros and cons of Dick Washington. David was right to be disturbed by Mike's question.

Mike felt Dick Washington was a scumbag, a womanizer with a reputation of ruthlessness. Washington sat on a number of boards in Chicago. Rumor had it he was a gambler and Mike was very much aware of other rumors that Washington had dealt from the bottom of the deck with suppliers and customers of Batem Communications. While none of this was first hand knowledge, he couldn't help wondering if Henry was aware of the rumor and innuendo surrounding his selection to captain the ship through these next perilous days. Not a chance, he thought to himself. As brilliant as Henry was about most matters, he was also extraordinarily loyal. What's more, Henry, though excellent at reading people and their agendas, had a difficult time seeing anything except the good in people. He often dismissed rumor and innuendo out of hand. Mike wondered if he should tell Henry. How could he? These were unsubstantiated rumors of the wildest kind.

While Mike was a kind, considerate, and gentlemanly person, being from Philly he still had contacts Henry couldn't even conceive of. He'd bide his time, he thought, and see how it played out.

CHAPTER 10

Ruth drove her husband to the hospital on Wednesday for his first chemotherapy session. Because the doctors were anticipating a reaction to the massive dose Henry would receive, they were going to keep him overnight. Depending on Henry's reaction to treatment, they would then decide on the next move.

Henry entered Rush-Presbyterian Hospital looking sickly and feeling low. He left three days later looking and feeling even worse. He had taken one chemo treatment and was violently ill. Vomiting had been his occupation for the past thirty-six hours, but the worst seemed past, and he was given respite for four days, when they would return for an even more potent round with the chemo. He had five more visits to contend with and then still faced heavy radiation. He now clearly understood why he had heard that if the cancer didn't kill you, the treatment for it might. He looked forward to rest and home.

Approaching their suburban Highland Park house, located on a bluff overlooking Lake Michigan, Ruth slowed the car as she turned into the driveway. When she came to a stop it was in front of the side garage, but she did not press the button that would have raised its door. Instead, with a thin smile on her face and all of the bravery she could gather, she asked Henry if it felt good to be home. There had been a noticeable silence in the car from the hospital to this point. Henry took a deep breath, turned his head, and held Ruth's hand. "It's going to be all right; it really is." A typical Henry answer she thought, concise and evasive. He told her only the good. He could be dying, which he was, and he would not want her to bother herself attending to his needs. His wife was a partner, a woman who shared in his life experiences. He felt comfortable discussing with her, and asking advise about, business decisions. He would not, however, involve her in anything unpleasant at any level, social, business or the very tiring process of dying.

A courageous man, and a giving man to his family, the community and to his Jewish heritage, Henry was determined to give his all to help ICA, his company, solve its succession problem before he died. The process started with the appointment of Dick

Washington as vice chair and interim president. He hoped he would get enough help from his medical treatments to effect a remission that would allow sufficient time for him to resolve the issue of a new permanent president and chairman. He desperately wanted that individual to come from within the culture of the company. An outsider would be a poor last resort. He knew that a chief executive brought from another company, even one within the life insurance industry, would perhaps never assimilate into the unusually consumer and employee friendly culture of ICA. An outsider would be the longest of long shots; but on the other hand, who from within the ranks of ICA had the abilities, charisma, and other attributes it would take to successfully run the company and retain its personality? He could think of none. Thinking was difficult with his mind clouded from medication and lack of sleep, but he had been tossing the problem around, and a few ideas were beginning to form in his mind. One of his thoughts kept coming back to a dark horse. Someone who had not surfaced before as a candidate in his mind, for a variety of reasons. Hour by hour the emergence of this individual seemed more and more possible to him. Still, he was far from sure or satisfied; his mind was so clouded by pain and discomfort, that as he stepped out of the car and Ruth came around to his side, he hoped at last his head would clear and he could think it all through.

Inside the comfortable home he was overwhelmed at how good he instantly began to feel in these familiar surroundings. His wife, pictures of the kids, his books, and not the least, the warm richness and comfort of his own bedroom and bed made him smile. His eyes grew moist. He had thought of moving his treatments to Highland Park Hospital, not more than a few minutes from home, but even though Rush was downtown and a schlep for Ruth, he wanted to be nearer to the office. Finally, in his pajamas, Henry looked about as Ruth fluffed a pillow behind him and he fingered a newspaper which he never picked up. Instead, tired beyond anything he could have imagined, he drifted into much needed sleep.

CHAPTER 11

It had been necessary for David to leave Chicago for a couple of days to attend an annual meeting with sales officers of other companies. They sat around a luxurious conference room in a fine hotel and shared their companies' problems and successes with each other. They also lied a lot and were careful to avoid giving away information of a proprietary nature. In the evening they had a reserved table at one of the city's finest dining establishments; their companies were paying, after all. This meeting was held in Scottsdale, Arizona, and David had not really gotten into it. More than one of his peers had inquired if he was feeling all right. He made up the typical flu bug story, mindful that all who had attended the executive meeting two weeks ago had agreed the real story had to be kept quiet until details had been resolved.

An announcement had been made to ICA employees which said only that Henry Rothblatt would be taking a leave of absence to recuperate from an illness, and further announcing the appointment of Dick Washington as vice chairman and interim president.

A meeting had been called by Boris Howe, ICA's Director of Public Relations, for tomorrow morning to discuss how to handle the situation with the media. The rating agencies would be interested as well and that would be crucial.

Hurrying from the meeting David boarded a plane at the Phoenix airport and moved into his first class seat, an upgrade. ICA paid for coach, but David traveled so extensively for both business and pleasure that he accumulated tons of air miles which he almost always used to upgrade his seat. Traveling light, he stowed his bag in the overhead and took off his sport coat folding it on top of the bag. He relaxed into his seat, his mind whirling with a million thoughts and was barely aware of the door to the plane closing. The big airliner began its taxi to a runway for takeoff.

David's first sense of something unusual was when he heard the voice of an attendant going through the usual preflight announce-ments. Sitting in the first row, at the bulkhead, in the window seat, David could not see the stewardess who was just finishing her spiel

29

with "welcome aboard." But he was suddenly on alert. The voice, who belonged to that voice? He tried hard to peek around the bulkhead but couldn't quite position himself. The woman sitting on David's left, on the aisle, prevented him from seeing the flight attendant who had just finished speaking. He was crazily mesmerized by that voice and an inner sense told him he had to see whom it belonged to.

Realizing that his sighting of the mystery stewardess with the mellifluous voice would have to wait until they were airborne, David relaxed, but only for a moment. Once again his senses suddenly became aroused. This time it was a smell. An odor, not pleasant at all, overwhelmed him. He couldn't quite place it or where it came from. Then, shit, he thought, it's her, the woman sitting next to him. Glancing in her direction, he saw, for the first time, a heavy-set woman in a navy dress with white polka dots. It had been hot, very hot, in Phoenix that day, and the material of her rayon dress smelled or else her deodorant had failed— whichever, it was unbearable.

All of the first class seats were occupied; there was nowhere to move; what in the hell was he going to do? The odor was awful and constant. For now it was grin and bear it, so he sat and looked out the window of the plane as it lifted off and began its three hour trip to Chicago. The smell, the odor, raged on endlessly, relentlessly. Suddenly his attention shifted from the smell to the most beautiful, angel-like face he had ever seen. David noticed that as she bent forward slightly to ask what he'd like to drink, her nose, a small, cute nose, wrinkled. She smelled it too. Oh Christ, he thought, I hope to hell she realizes it's the woman and not me that smells. Just to make certain he wrinkled his nose and pinched it with his fingers making certain he did so out of range of the woman's line of sight. The beautiful face broke into an involuntary laugh and, at that instant, a glass of water on the tray she was holding tipped and spilled. Most of its contents dripped onto the smelly woman. There was a stunned silence as all three watched the water trickle and dribble from her lap tray onto her dress. David covered his eyes in mock horror. The stewardess with the beautiful face could just barely contain herself from laughing at him and backed away amid her stammered apologies. She reappeared in a few seconds with hand towels to soak up the water from her passenger's lap, knees, and legs. Through it all, the woman sat still as a board, unmoving, and David could not take his eyes from those of the lovely young stewardess.

David and the girl each felt suddenly and strangely uncomfortable, but each quickly regained their composure. As the stewardess disappeared into the first class galley, David offered a sincere "too bad" to the woman next to him and picked up a magazine. He held it upside down, as he thought only of when the gorgeous face might reappear.

David had no way of knowing that the stewardess was thinking of every way possible to make contact with him. She was constrained in this by her desire to remain lady-like and, even more so, because her duties kept her busy. David's seating assignment kept him isolated from her during most of the flight. At O'Hare he would be one of the first off the plane; the stewardess would, of course, be one of the last. She told herself that she somehow had to keep him in sight and make contact.

When the flight landed and taxied to its gate, the usual exiting chaos took place. Passengers elbowed their way from their seats to the aisle and forward to the front of the cabin. The pretty stewardess was stationed at the front door in order to bid each of them goodbye. She still had not figured out how she would somehow make contact with the good-looking young man who had caught her attention in seat 1A. His chiseled face had her acting like a schoolgirl and, although intellectually she knew it, she couldn't control herself.

Passengers were exiting and although she was certain he would be next, she didn't see him until the plane had nearly emptied. When she looked up, there was a grinning, handsome man looking younger than his actual age of thirty-seven, and he was staring at her. As he slowly approached her, she could not help the sly smile that crept onto her face. David thought that smile was all at once sexy, demure, and most definitely worthwhile getting to know. Standing next to him she said nothing. As she put her jacket over her blouse, she stretched her arm and he could not help but notice her breasts, which were most pleasant to look at. He was not certain if she prolonged the process to afford him a better look. Finally he said, "If you live here in Chicago, and I hope you do, but even if not, please call me if you'd like to have a drink." He handed her a business card. She took it and wrote something on its back. Then she handed it back to him.

"Lisa," she said, "my name is Lisa and this is my number in Chicago. I'd like it if you called me."

"Well, Lisa, I'll call soon. I can't wait to find out your last name." She smiled. "Bye, bye. Thanks for flying with us."

CHAPTER 12

Henry had returned to Rush for treatment and, as he expected, it was even rougher than the first round. A fifteen pound weight loss accentuated his normally lean frame. David and others visited by phone and in person. All of them found it extraordinary that he maintained his interest for everything connected with ICA. He knew that Dick Washington had inserted himself into the company's day in and day out activities and that he was learning more about the company on a daily basis. Henry still was thinking through his nomination of a new permanent president for the company. Eventually he felt he would be able to resume his activities as chairman so that he could work with a new CEO for a couple of years. At seventy he would face mandatory retirement. Of course, he kept telling himself, all of this assumed he lived that long. He could replace himself as chairman with the same person he hoped would assume the presidency of the company. Getting well and back to work was uppermost in Henry's mind, and he was religious in following Dr. Weinstein's protocol. He could deal with the diarrhea and vomiting, even the pain, but the constant weariness was wearing. But this man was tenacious, and he wanted to get back into the ICA saddle a.s.a.p. Each day the weariness interrupted his plans, and he would fall into a deep sleep. When he would awaken he was not refreshed physically, really, but at least he was prepared mentally for a few more gritty hours.

Dick Washington, in the meantime, was enjoying his new role and was totally energized. He called Dena at the university and they made a date for drinks at 5:30 that afternoon. The Pump Room is a famous restaurant in the Ambassador East Hotel, where for years celebrities visiting Chicago would meet to be seen sitting in Booth One. It's where Irv Kupcinet, the famous *Sun Times* columnist and one of Chicago's favorite sons, would nightly gather items for his syndicated column. After a slump, the Pump Room restaurant and bar had been restored to its original luster by the Lettuce Entertain You group headed by a brash, but brilliant young man, Rich Melman. The room now catered to a middle-aged crowd of mostly singles or

33

business travelers at the bar. Chicagoans frequented the dining room and, in particular, loved to sit at the window tables looking out at North State Parkway.

The restaurant was located only a block from Richard's home. He was entranced by Dena, but today he wanted to meet with her about a serious business matter. The scheme he wanted to discuss with her had an erotic rhythm to it all of its own.

After she had given the doorman her car, she entered the Ambassador East lobby, walked up a few steps and past a sentimental display of 1950 to 1970 celebrity photographs—Cary Grant, Don Rickles, Marilyn Monroe. She strolled past their photos toward Dick who was sitting at a small cabaret table near the railing that separated the bar from the dining room.

She was fifteen minutes late thought Washington as he eyed the beautiful woman walking confidently toward him. He could not help wondering how anyone with such grace and a body that didn't quit could also possess one of the foremost financial minds in the country. He noticed her business suit. Damn, he said to himself. He desperately wanted to get a good look at her breasts which were covered by an Armani double-breasted jacket. He also, however, desperately wanted to share his idea with her and watch her reaction.

"Hi, beautiful." He smiled at her and reached for her hand to help her into a chair. "Traffic?" he asked.

"The Drive was a madhouse around the Field Museum," she replied.

"Let me get you a drink; I want you to relax."

Smiling demurely, she said, "I thought this was going to be business," and at that instant she pressed her knee into his under the table.

"It is, it is." He pulled his leg from hers. He needed to concentrate and really did want her reaction to his thoughts regarding ICA. "You know," he began, "I've spent a couple of weeks at the ICA offices now, mostly getting to know people and letting them talk. They've told me about their roles and shared their perspective on the company."

The waiter arrived and brought the gin martini he had ordered for her. "It's been very interesting," he went on. "Have you looked closely at ICA's financials recently?"

She took a sip of her cocktail as she pulled a cigarette from her purse. He took a stick match from a box on the table, struck it, and helped her light the long white cylinder. He was mesmerized by her slender fingers and long red polished nails. As he looked into her eyes he was struck by their sensuousness. He had to quickly bring himself back to the moment, and continued, "ICA is a cash cow. The company turns a profit one year after another, and I'm talking about amazing profits. They're doing it in spite of an executive board and officers that don't know their asses from a hole in the ground. The damn company runs itself. The beautiful thing is they have several separate profit centers. No matter what the economic environment or situation, one division or another is going to pull the company through to another record year. It's absolutely amazing; a shoe store would be harder to operate."

"Generally, I'm aware of all of that," Dena commented, "but what about it? I mean, so what? The only ones who really profit are the policyholders who own the company through their rights. Henry's done a marvelous job building the company; he's a genius, but so what?"

"All right," Dick Washington intoned. "Let me go through this slowly and see if the light goes on for you as it so brightly has for me. We have an immensely profitable company which practically runs itself. Other than Henry, we have inept, naive management, who babble on all day about ICA's culture. Talk to them about a new president and it could be Donald Duck, as far as they're concerned. Just as long as Donald retains the culture." Washington was warming to the task. "This culture, incidentally, is based not on a culture of profitability but on some stupid notion that they are all caretakers of the policyholders funds. My God, they have a rate of return on their investments of only about 6 percent. They don't know the meaning of the word risk. And finally, we have a chairman of the board who is incapacitated, out of it. The genius of Henry Rothblatt lies in a hospital bed, delusional, weak, and hardly able to communicate. Now, what does all that suggest, Dena?"

35

As the beautiful woman took another drink from her glass, this time she sucked on it down to the ice. She peered at Dick over the brim of the glass, stared really, and slowly lowered it. Those sexy eyes were dazzling with light. He knew she had made the connection, seen the light. It truly was an erotic experience, he thought, as she finally spoke the words. In fact she spit the words out and he thought he saw sparks fly from her mouth. She said, "Take over!"

CHAPTER 13

A short, slight, boyish look belied his abilities; Boris Howe was a nice man and a gay man. His lifestyle, however, had nothing whatsoever to do with his work and did not interfere in any way with the fact that he was a talented public relations specialist. As the head of ICA's Public Relations Department, Boris would naturally handle any routine announcements regarding ICA's appointment of a temporary vice chairman and interim president.

David, Tim Walker, Daryl Green, and Bob Wellington were already present, along with Boris, in the small conference room on the seventieth floor of the ICA Building where Boris' office and the Public Relations Department were located. "Is Dick Washington going to be attending?" asked David.

"No, I don't think so," answered Boris. "He said he felt this was something we could handle and to shout if we felt we needed his assistance."

Boris explained that he had two agendas. First, the company would have to satisfy the general public's need to know and that would include the policyholders. The second group to satisfy was the insurance community at large and the rating agencies in particular. "The rating agencies," snapped Bob Wellington. "Blasted agencies are like big brother, every damn thing we do around here requires their fucking approval."

Wellington was not altogether wrong. Until the late 1980s, A.M. Best Company had a monopoly on offering financial ratings to life insurance companies. The general feeling of those who knew was that a favorable rating from A.M. Best was not very difficult to acquire. If an insurance company asked and paid for a rating, subscribed to their other services, and were reasonably sound fiscally, or at least looked like they were on the surface, it was thought a favorable "A" or "A+" rating could be easily secured. In the nineties all of that changed. With the recession and subsequent failing of several life insurance companies led by the Executive Life fiasco and later by the bankruptcy of Mutual Benefit Life, the major rating agencies—Moodys, Duff & Phelps, Standard and Poor—all saw the life insurance industry as fertile ground.

Why had A.M. Best not been able to predict the failure of Executive Life and other companies? They simply had not looked hard enough into the right areas of concern. The consensus was that they had not done quality due diligence. The larger rating agencies would not make the same mistakes, but the bigger agencies did not know the life insurance industry. They would find it to be very different, but not different enough, to be held to another standard. The industry would have to be measured by the same monitoring and would have to stand up fiscally to any other industry or financial institution.

The death of Executive Life and Mutual Benefit along with the financial weakening of other giants of the business, such as Connecticut Mutual and New England Life, came about principally through investments that were too risky.

The appearance of variable rates of return on life insurance policies and annuities started a war of interest rates for new business. A pissing contest began over which company would pay its clients the largest return on their cash values. In order to achieve higher rates, many companies committed funds to risky investments, especially in commercial real estate. When those investments got into trouble during the eighties, companies could not bail out fast enough and huge losses resulted. Most could sustain the losses; a few could not. ICA held no appreciable commercial property other than its Home Office building at the time of the 1987 crash. Henry Rothblatt was looked at as a genius for ridding the company of its commercial real estate holdings prior to that time and avoiding losses to the ICA bottom line.

Of equal importance, Henry was committed to investment quality. His commitment was so strong he would not allow, and ICA did not play, the interest rate game. Henry mapped out a strategy of selling the company's financial strength and its ability to deliver on its promises. "A life insurance policy is a promise to pay," he would say. "Let's remain certain ICA will always be able to deliver on its promises."

David did a magnificent job getting his sales force to buy the idea, which was no easy task. Sales people being sales people would have liked to have been able to talk about high interest rates and compete with those companies that zeroed in on a marketing strategy of talking phenomenal returns. David, in short order, actually had his sales force selling against high interest rates by equating them with high risk. ICA, David would point out, proposed lower, more sensible rates, and that meant safety and the ability to deliver on promises. It was a brilliant strategy, and once the rating agencies saw that ICA's agents had the company on a record sales course, they saw the company, under Henry's leadership, as being on the right track, and then some. The strategy paid off in strong financial ratings. As always, David incorporated Mike Spellari into the plan, and, as usual, Mike delivered by endorsing the idea, first to his own agents and then to his peers nationally, throughout the ICA field force.

Bob Wellington nudged David as Boris was talking and whispered, "Hey buddy, have you had any meetings or talks with Washington yet? Strange guy, isn't he?"

"Do you think so?" David asked.

"Wait 'til he gives you his cash cow theory. You'll see. By the way, did you know this company could be run just like a shoe store with little management and still be quite successful?"

David looked at Wellington quizzically. "You'll see," Bob said.

When the meeting had ended with agreement that Boris would handle all of the details of Henry's illness and Dick Washington's role insofar as PR was concerned, David walked slowly to his office reading a sales report but not really seeing it. What the hell was Wellington talking about, he wondered. He decided to talk more with Bob and find out what his conversation with Dick Washington had really been about.

CHAPTER 14

Mike Spellari arrived at his office located on Erie Street just east of Michigan Avenue and only a few blocks from ICA's home office. He had chosen this location for four reasons. First, it was close to several hospitals including Northwestern, and therefore was easily accessible to doctors with whom his agents did a lot of business. Ask any life insurance agent and they will readily explain that most doctors are seen as financial imbeciles. Physicians, in general, knew little about insurance or investing and were especially weak at discerning risk. As a group, Mike supposed physicians were at the top of the list of those who had made poor investment choices over the years. This meant they needed the professional assistance of Mike's corps of financial planners.

The second reason for choosing the Erie Street location was its proximity to ICA. Mike's peers were amazed at the number of times he talked the company into providing a favor such as a break in underwriting a case, and at how quickly his people could get something done. They failed to take into account that Mike received those breaks not just because of his proximity to ICA but because his was the company's largest sales agency. Being in Chicago and playing off their name recognition didn't hurt, of course.

His third reason for choosing Erie Street, was that Mike was able to recruit sales people from all parts of the city and suburbs. Chicago has three sides, north, south, and west; the east side is Lake Michigan. Centrally located in the downtown area Mike could recruit from the breadth of the greater city; in the suburbs the agency would have been pretty much restricted in recruiting good sales people.

The fourth and final reason was the office's proximity to the downtown CPA's and lawyers who helped the doctors and others that Mike and his agents dealt with to reach decisions.

There was actually a fifth reason for Erie Street. Mike was a city person and loved the inner city which is why he and his family chose to live there. It meant private schools for his kids, but it also meant the excitement that the energy of the city brings. A walk down Michigan Avenue on a warm, sunny, spring day was invigorating.

The stores, the beautiful women, the restaurants—Mike loved it all. The office's location and the various city activities also gave Mike the opportunity to know and mix with Chicago's "in" crowd, a combination of successful people that included politicians, business owners, and even a few "crooked noses". The latter was Mike's term for those that moved on Chicago's seamier side. It was through these contacts that Mike stayed abreast of what was really happening in the city—forget what the <u>Sun</u> <u>Times</u> or <u>Tribune</u> said. It was through these contacts that he had heard the stories about Dick Washington. The most persistent story was that Dick had really not retired from Batem Electronics. There appeared to be more to it than that, but Mike couldn't get a handle on the real facts. The fact that Dick had a reputation as a womanizer was enough in itself to cause a staunch Italian Catholic like Mike to be put off. Mike was a stand-up guy to whom loyalty meant everything, including family and wife.

The phone rang as he was about to pour himself a cup of black coffee and begin his morning routine of opening mail and listening to messages. He removed the receiver and was pleasantly surprised to hear David's voice.

"You run this morning?" David asked.

"No, the knees are hurting," replied Mike. "What's going on at ICA today?"

"Not much but we had a PR meeting yesterday to discuss how we wanted to handle releasing all the news, and during the meeting Bob Wellington made a few strange comments to me about a visit he had with Washington."

"Really?" replied Mike. "Like what?"

"Oh, I don't know, stuff about ICA being a cash cow; a bunch of vague comments really. I'm going to visit with Bob today and try to get him to be a little clearer, but I can tell you that I didn't like the tone of it at all."

Mike gave David still more to think about when he said, "Well, I've heard a few things too, mostly about Dick Washington's so-called retirement from Batem. I'm not in love with what I'm hearing either."

"Hey, why don't we go over to the hospital and see Henry this afternoon?" said David. "We'll have lunch and try to cheer him up, and then you and I can have a talk, say about 12:30?"

"I'll be there." David hung up the phone and picked it back up to see if he could schedule some time with Wellington. He hoped he had misunderstood Bob's comments about Washington.

CHAPTER 15

As David stepped off the elevator on his way to Bob Wellington's office, he caught Nancy Wagner's eye as she sat at her desk guarding Henry's office. He wondered what she was doing to keep herself busy while Henry was away. He thought briefly that she looked somewhat preoccupied. He and Nancy were kindred spirits when it came to their love of Henry Rothblatt. He knew this was a sad time for her. She wasn't married, and while she was an outwardly happy woman, David sometimes thought about what her life was like away from ICA. He thought it must be boring and quiet. Nancy was plain and stout; she looked older than she actually was, and being unmarried, he again thought she must be lonely. Then he thought about his own situation; was he lonely? He remembered the stewardess, Lisa, and made a mental note to call her.

Before he could contemplate either his own or Nancy's love life any further, he found himself inside the Legal Department. He didn't really remember pushing the door open to the reception area too and he thought Nancy was preoccupied too. Bob Wellington was just returning from the rest room, and when he saw David, he put his large right arm around his shoulder and pulled him to his side. "Come on in, buddy boy." David had been in Bob's office many times, usually to discuss a problem with a disgruntled policyholder or, unfortunately, an agent gone bad. More often than not, the agent's problem was one born from a mistake. On occasion, however, and much to David's chagrin, he found that a particular act was intentional and designed to benefit the agent's pocketbook at the expense of a client. On those occasions, Bob helped David to understand the legal consequences of an agent's action so he could deal with it.

As they sat in a typical attorney's office, disorganized looking, David looked at the big man and asked for an explanation of the remarks Bob had attributed to Washington. "This guy is wacko, David. It's not exactly a legal term, but it's an accurate one." David didn't speak, but the look of puzzlement on his face prompted Wellington to continue. "He came to see me as part of a plan to visit with senior VP's to find out what he could about their particular areas

43

of the company. That made sense to me, so I welcomed his call and cleared my calendar to see him at his convenience."

David was waiting for his host to get to the meat. He squirmed a bit in his seat in front of Bob's desk, but the big man paid little attention as he continued to set up his conversation with Dick Washington. "He started our visit by telling me how he had always found lawyers to be obstructionists, but he was certain we'd get along. Then, instead of asking a single question, he started this diatribe. ICA was a company totally out of step with the mainstream financial and business community. His research, whatever that amounted to, showed him that the company was basically a cash cow; the money keeps coming in no matter what we do. Why, we could close our doors to the sale of new business and, if we simply concentrated on maintaining the business on the books, cut expenses, and invested wisely, we would be way ahead financially. When I questioned cutting expenses, he told me the company would no longer have to foot the expense of a full-blown legal department with all the high salaries and a bunch of guys who sit on their asses making trouble. When I asked about his so-called research, he was evasive. When I pointed out that our culture is made up of serving and protecting people and that our goal is to do that while simultaneously providing quality employment for a lot of people, he exploded. He said culture was of no concern to him or the board—profits were."

David was stunned. He found what he was hearing almost unbelievable. Bob Wellington was a good lawyer, and definitely not prone to exaggeration. "Bob," he said, "what do we do? This guy is a friend of Henry's, someone Henry knows well, and he has Henry's endorsement. What in the hell do we do about him?"

"I don't know," Bob replied. "Believe me, I haven't thought about much else. Maybe you'll get a call and visit with him yourself. Then we should talk some more. In the meantime, I think we keep this to ourselves, though I will tell you that I shared my conversation with Tim, who had already gotten a call. I think Tim and this asshole met this morning at breakfast. You may want to see how their meeting turned out."

David agreed to contact Tim and that they should keep their talk between themselves. He knew he would share what he had learned with Mike, and that reminded him it was time to head for the hospital to meet with him and see Henry. After a handshake, David left and headed back to his own office to grab his raincoat. The Chicago sky was hazy and a cold mist hung over the city. David hoped, against hope, that it did not portend things to come.

CHAPTER 16

Ruth sat facing the door of the hospital room with a blanket wrapped around her legs. It wasn't particularly cold or chilly but from the window of Henry's room she could see the gray sky and rain, and it felt cooler than it actually was. It was May, and Chicago seldom had a definitive spring; either it was unseasonably warm or cold; rain was common, and it had been coming down for a couple of days now.

When Mike and David arrived at Henry's room, the door was open. They saw Ruth, who looked up. Henry was asleep; he looked frail and clammy but seemed to be breathing smoothly. Ruth threw aside her blanket, stood up, and held her finger to her lips as she moved toward them, and they walked together through the door and into the hospital's corridor. At 1:30 in the afternoon it was slow, lunch had been served and trays had been picked up. Rounds were long over, medicines dispensed, and patients had been moved about and returned to their rooms. The staff could now spend time directing the traffic of visitors and answering questions. They also looked forward to the end of their shifts or the end of visiting hours, whichever came first.

The three of them, Mike, David, and Ruth, moved to the wall across from Henry's room. "Boys, it's so nice to see you. Henry is doing fine. The treatment this time was much tougher, but he did tolerate it and is starting to gain back some strength. The doctors are keeping him here a couple of extra days just to be sure."

"What about you, hon?" asked David. "Are you okay?"

"Yes, yes, just fine. The kids take good care of us both," Ruth answered.

"We just came by to say hello to Henry, but we don't want to wake him," said Mike. "Hey, how about some lunch? David and I are going to grab a sandwich in the cafeteria. Come on, a cup of coffee will do you good."

"No, I just want to sit and be here when he awakens. Why don't the two of you go down and bring me back some tea? Maybe Henry will be awake when you return." David and Mike agreed and headed to the elevator descending to the hospital's basement where the cafeteria was located. After going through a line which was mercifully short, they sat at a table, sandwiches and diet Cokes in front of them.

"Did you find out anything from Wellington?" asked Mike.

"Just an elaboration on what he had told me before. I do have a date to see Tim, who met with Washington at breakfast this morning."

"I sure don't like the way this deal is shaping up," Mike said. "Washington is a snake in the grass. Who knows what damage he'll do before Henry can get back."

"If he gets back!" David retorted.

"Do you really think it's that bad?"

"Mike, all I know is esophageal cancer is deadly and quick. Henry's chosen some intensive treatments just to try to extend his life. He doesn't have any thoughts about beating it."

"Shit."

"Yeah, shit," agreed David. "It's crap all the way around. Henry loses; we lose; ICA loses."

There was a prolonged silence between the two men before Mike spoke again. "You know, David, Washington may be thinking he wants to turn all of our losses into a win for himself."

"But how?" asked David.

"Well, Dick Washington is our new leader, for the moment anyway, but I have the uncomfortable feeling he may try to make it permanent. If he does, he may attempt to turn ICA into his own personal profit center." David listened to Mike but tempered what he had heard with the thought that his friend had a habit of seeing conspiracies everywhere.

"Look, Mike, Washington may be a jerk, but he's smart and he knows there are limits to his power. The executive committee will see to it he learns what we're all about, and even if they fail, the board will rein him in."

"Take a close look at that board, David. Aside from Callahan, who, word has it, sleeps with the bastard, the board is vulnerable. Most of them don't know the first thing about our company. They've been a rubber stamp for Henry who, thank God, is honest and caring

47

as the day is long. But they can learn to rubber stamp Washington too. In their eyes he's Henry's hand-picked apostle. They know him as successful, and the head of one of the most prestigious business schools in the country will endorse whatever he proposes. No, good buddy, they'll buy in and go along."

As they sat silently picking at their sandwiches, Mike finally broke the silence by trying to lighten things up. "Hey, have you met with that 'stew' you told me about?"

"Damn," David shot out. "With everything that's been going on, I completely forgot about her until this morning. Well, not exactly forgot, I just haven't had the time to call her."

They were still discussing David's stewardess as they got out of the elevator and headed for Henry's room. "You really should give her a call, it would do you a world of good to find some good company. You're getting stale, you know, all work and no play. Call her," urged Mike.

"Call who?" asked Ruth overhearing the end of their conversation. "A woman, I hope."

"You too," squeaked David.

"Me too if we're talking about finding you a young lady." Mike and David looked up somewhat startled. It was Henry, sitting up in bed, and though he was thin and gaunt, he looked wonderful to them.

"He awoke about thirty minutes ago and said he felt fine. He wants to know when he can go home," said Ruth.

"As soon as I can sign the order," said Dr. Weinstein, poking his head in the door. "I told you Henry was ill from the treatment, not so much from the disease. Now it looks like he's coming around. Just let me check him over. If he's as good as he says and looks, we'll send him home and let him rest there. I'll be back in about twenty minutes."

"I'm fine, and you need a woman, David." Henry looked at Mike with a serious face. "With all your connections in this city, can't you find a nice girl for him?"

"Believe me, Henry, I've tried. My wife and I have fixed him up a dozen times, but a loser is a loser. Seems our man David just can't make the grade."

"I don't believe it for a second," Ruth interrupted. "David has what every woman wants, looks, personality, and he's a good person."

"Ruth, you sound like my mother, keep going," laughed David.

"Well, who is this woman you're supposed to be calling?" Henry questioned.

"Just a gorgeous, red-headed stewardess who looks like Meg Ryan and has a smile that puts our man into orbit," said Mike.

"Well, why not call her, dear?" asked Ruth.

"Hey, have I lost control here, or what? I'll call her. I'll call her. Now, can we please visit with Henry? That's why we came here."

"I don't need any visiting; I'm getting out of here. I feel good. With a little home rest, I'll be able to spend a few days in the office before the next treatment. Have you boys met with Dick yet?"

"Not me," replied Mike. "But I'm just a lowly sales manager."

"I'm calling him this afternoon to set up a meeting; hopefully he and I can meet tomorrow," said David.

"Good, and while you're making that call, remember to call your young lady. Then let me have a report on both meetings."

"Henry, you'll want the family-rated version, I hope," chipped in Mike. They all smiled, and after hugging Henry, Mike and David departed, each heading back to his own office. Ruth stayed on and waited for the return of Dr. Weinstein. She held Henry's hand and he let her. It comforted him to know she was there and he couldn't get enough of her intuitively knowing that, no matter how well he felt today, there was not too much time left.

Mike and David left each other at the hospital door after agreeing they would talk after David's meeting with Washington.

49

CHAPTER 17

The window they stood in front of overlooked, to their left, Marina Towers with its odd circular shape. Its twin spirals reflected their light upon the water of the Chicago River, while to their right were the locks separating the river from Lake Michigan.

Having met earlier for cocktails, they took a cab to Ambria, a small, pricey, restaurant with elegant food and service. Their conversation had only touched on business and was laced with secret laughter, double entendre, and sexual innuendo. When they finished with the soufflé and drained the last drop of amaretto, they again took a cab and headed to the Hyatt Regency where Richard had reserved a room. Earlier in the day, he had discretely pre-registered so they simply alit from their yellow taxi and ventured directly to the elevators and their room. As they traversed the lobby, they looked like what they were—a couple with a devil-may-care attitude, thumbing their noses at the world.

In their room, Washington took Dena's coat and hung it in the hallway closet. Then with the key to the mini-bar in hand, he offered to pour a drink for her. "Vino," she said, and he proceeded to pour from a small bottle of red wine he found on the inside door of the bar. They held their glasses and looked out from the window high atop the hotel. He slipped an arm around her waist from behind and kissed her neck and behind her ear.

"Richard, what's the next move?"

"To the bed, of course," he responded.

"No, silly, with regard to ICA. What do we do next to take control and make all of us a lot of money?"

He knew exactly what she had meant but he didn't know which excited him more, the idea of a take-over at ICA and its resulting windfall or his urgent need for her. He wanted her intensely, having spent the last few hours looking at her, smelling her, being next to her. This wasn't love for Richard, not even close. He never gave it much thought, but deep inside he knew he was not truly capable of love. His needs were money and gratified lust. He had originally married for both, now only the money remained.

While he wanted to arouse her and be aroused, he didn't mind discussing ICA. Standing next to her, his hand cupping a breast, the finger tracing a nipple lightly through the thin fabric of her dress, talking with her about the ICA deal gave him almost unbearable pleasure.

"You and I, my sweet, will begin a little campaign to educate our fellow board members, but it will be subtle. We'll offer a much better understanding of ICA and educate our directors. It will seem as though we're giving them a pep talk but, in reality, we'll be setting them up. During the course of their education, they'll get a chance to see how ICA operates, from our perspective, of course. We'll introduce them to the ICA culture and that culture's true cost. If we do our job right, they will first think in terms of reforms, but we'll step in very quickly and show them that would be a mistake. Ultimately, they'll want a total change, especially when they realize the tremendous financial opportunity for each of them if we take ICA public."

As Richard spoke and, as he began pinching her nipple, Dena felt herself start to perspire and her knees became weak. She pressed back into him feeling his hardness. They were still both fully dressed.

She turned her face around toward his and asked, "When do we start?"

"Now," he said and turned her fully toward him. They kissed, tongues challenging each other. She began loosening his belt. He unbuttoned her dress. Soon each wore only their undergarments—she in bra and panties, he in boxer shorts. As he pushed her into a large soft chair, he bent to his knees putting one of her legs over each of his shoulders. He pressed forward and kissed the cleanly shaven mound through her panties. Dena leaned back into the chair and, at his direction began holding and caressing her own breasts, still within her bra.

The two of them acted as though at the center of a hurricane—no love, just the need for gratification. It was strong, it was brutal; each seemed to push ahead for more, moving to the bed, panting, swearing, pinching, hitting, pulling, and pushing. When it was over, they lay exhausted, separately, in the bed.

"I'll call George Walker tomorrow," she said, once calmed.

CHAPTER 18

At 5:30 A.M. David's alarm sounded and he hit the snooze button. The action would allow him another ten minutes of sleep before the thing went off again. He closed his eyes but within just a few seconds, he opened them again too pumped up to fall back asleep. His mind began to race ahead thinking about his breakfast with Dick Washington this morning. He had telephoned Dick yesterday afternoon after returning to his office. He told Washington a white lie: "I'm leaving town for a few days and heard you were trying to visit with most of the senior VP's. I thought I'd give you a buzz and see if you wanted to talk about the individual sales organization," he had said to Dick.

"Yes, yes indeed, I've heard quite a bit about you, David, all of it good. You bet I'd like to visit and get your thoughts. I also want to share a few of my own with you."

"Well fine, Dick, how about breakfast? Henry and I usually meet at the East Bank."

Washington said, "I prefer the grill at the Wrigley Building, David, just habit, I guess. Is that okay with you, say 7:30 tomorrow morning?"

David didn't hesitate. "You're on, 7:30 at the Wrigley Grill. I'll see you in the morning."

Usually David liked to research his prey, but last evening when he sat down to see what he knew, or could find out, about Richard Washington, he realized how little he really did know. Washington had been in banking most of his career. Then ten years ago he was hired as chief financial officer at Batem Electronics, a New York Stock Exchange company. Four years ago he had been named president and CEO and remained so until recently when, at the age of only fifty-five, he had retired. Under his leadership the company's stock had an extraordinary run up. He was married, didn't have kids; his wife came from a pile of money and, from what he could tell, David was reasonably certain, given Dick's reputation, that the marriage, whatever it was to begin with, had turned into one of convenience. Dick Washington fooled around, of that David was certain. He also seemed to travel a lot and word was he would gamble on what time the sun would rise.

David knew that at age fifty-five Dick would have a relatively small pension. Of course, there may have been, make that for certain there was, a severance package. He wondered if Mrs. Washington was letting him fool around on her and funding his extravagant lifestyle too? He had not even met the man yet somehow he disliked him.

As he looked into the mirror and shaved, David thought about the two questions he really needed answered: What were Washington's plans for ICA, and what did Washington think was going to happen to keep Henry Rothblatt from eventually putting the company into appropriate hands. Henry had named Dick as interim president and vice chairman, but Henry Rothblatt controlled everything. That thought caused an involuntary smile to appear on David's face. Yet another thought crossed David's mind as he finished at the mirror and put on a new pale blue dress shirt. Lisa, he had to call her. It had been over two weeks and he had not found the time. He wrote himself a note and placed it in his cash pocket. He would have his breakfast with Dick and then call Lisa. Lisa, with no last name. Lisa, with the smile of his life. What a day this is going to be, he thought.

When he arrived by cab at the Wrigley Building, he walked through the revolving doors, turned to his left and through another door leading him into the grill. He immediately saw Dick Washington sitting at a table. Why, the bastard had already ordered and was eating! Son of a bitch. It's not as though David had been late. To the contrary, he was a few minutes early. Washington signaled with his hand for David to sit and he did. A napkin was tucked into Dick Washington's shirt protecting both his shirt and his red flowered tie. A cigarette was burning in an ashtray. "Hope you don't mind that I got started, big day today." You too, David thought. "Lots to do, places to go, people to see, including you, young man. You seem to be a bright and shining star at ICA. Tell me, David, why not you? Why wouldn't Henry Rothblatt look in your direction for a new president at ICA?"

Whew, thought David, this guy doesn't waste any time. "Mr.

Washington, Dick, I'm a very good sales executive. What I know about running an insurance company or financial services company, as we now like to be called, is negligible. Great salesman, lousy financier. I think that about sums it up."

"Well, I have great plans for ICA, and you're a part of them, and I'm not yet convinced you wouldn't make a damn fine president for this company. Shit, you don't have to be any kind of genius to run this company. Why it basically runs itself."

Bingo, this is what Bob Wellington was talking about. "David, ICA is a sleeping giant; almost without regard for any actions we take, money just keeps rolling in the front door. ICA is a goddamned cash cow, and we need to make better use of the money. We have to cut and trim upper management and rank and file as well. I keep hearing talk about ICA's culture. Well, culture be damned. What we need to talk about is the bottom line. I know ICA's line is very good for a mutual insurance company, but we've got to improve it so that it's good whether we're an insurance company, bank or shoe store. If 5 percent return is good for a mutual insurance company, then we've got to increase it to 15 percent because that's what's good for most businesses. We've got to cut costs and still grow; we need to raise capital and position ourselves for the future. And David, you can be an integral part of the plan. We'll need young, bold leadership, and from all I've heard, you can give ICA just that."

"Dick, I truly appreciate your feelings about me, but it seems a little fast. I've got lots of questions and a few thoughts of my own. First of all, it sounds very much like you're talking about a plan to take ICA public and demutalize it."

"Exactly, demutalize," shot back Washington. "See, you know more than you think, young man." The waiter suddenly appeared over David's shoulder for his breakfast order. David indicated he wanted no food, just black coffee, and once the waiter walked away he continued.

"Dick, I know what you propose sounds pretty good in theory. My question is, good for whom, and what will Henry have to say about all of this? Cutting jobs means cutting services. Henry will take a loss of employees' jobs and a loss of policyholder services very personally. Demutalization has many faces and one of them is loss of control to the people who are now the owners of ICA, its policy-holders. Henry believes in the company's promises, one of which is ownership rights to each policyholder. Profits are important, but they are only one factor in measuring how we're doing; they're not the only yardstick we use. As far as culture, well, I wouldn't want to be the one to demean this company's culture to Henry Rothblatt. The history, the promises made, the fairness in how we treat each other and our clients, those are all a part of the culture.

"As for me, as president of this company, well, that's just not going to happen. I don't want it to happen because I'm not the right man for the job, but then I suppose that's why Henry will ultimately make that decision. He'll pick the right man. My understanding is that you were named as interim president and interim vice chairman of the board, and I understand your appointment is temporary, at Henry's will. I also understood you were Henry's friend; in that I was obviously misled. You've managed to upset a number of people with your cash cow rhetoric. I would suggest you enjoy your interim position; you'll be back in your own world very soon."

"Why you punk!" Richard Washington was seething. His hands were shaking with rage as he stood up from his chair alongside the breakfast table. David thought he might leap across the table. When Washington looked around and realized others were glancing in his direction, he sat back down. Between clinched teeth he whispered, "You son of a bitch, I serve you up with the opportunity of a lifetime, a chance for you to make millions, and you smart talk me? Well, Mr. Hotshot, let me tell you a few things. To start with, within a few days I may no longer be an interim or vice anything. What's more, you'll find yourself out on your ass without Henry Rothblatt to run inter-ference for you. The best you'll be able to do will be to get a job selling this shit you peddle. I'm sick and tired of your fucking culture, and as for my personal friendship with Rothblatt, it was bad enough I had a Jew for a neighbor, I certainly don't want to share a company with him."

With that, Washington stood up, signed the check that had earlier been placed on the table, and strode defiantly out of the room. David sat very still. It was as though he had just taken a bad fall and wanted to check and be certain of no broken bones. He knew now he was either going to be shortly out of a job or he and ICA were in for one hell of a fight. He needed to get hold of Mike so they could put their heads together. He also thought it might be wise to call a meeting of the executive committee. As he stood and looked at the door that led out of the restaurant and onto Michigan Avenue, he noticed a bank of pay phones. He didn't have his cellular with him. He looked at his watch—8:45. Wow, that's the fastest moving breakfast meeting he could ever recall. It seemed to him their meeting had taken only a few minutes. Oh well, time flies when you're having fun, he thought.

David took some change from his suit jacket pocket. He removed a piece of paper, glanced at it, then dropped the coins into the phone and dialed. He heard her answering machine. At last he spoke, "Lisa, this is David Rourke. I know I should have called a lot sooner, but the bottom line is that I'm dying to find out your last name."

CHAPTER 19

During the next few weeks, Dick and Dena began meeting one on one with ICA board members. They were subtle in their approach, just as they had discussed; they made no derogatory remarks, rather, it was "poor Henry." At the same time, however, they planted seeds, letting each board member know that the company might have to face going on without Henry's leadership.

They had agreed that the real focus of their discussions with board members should be aimed at convincing them that now was the right time to appoint a new president. Henry, even if he returned, would never be able to continue in the dual role of president and chairman. Who the new president would be had to be carefully thought out. Their feeling was that Henry had no one specific in mind. They reasoned that if he had, his selection would have surfaced by now. They also knew that each board member had been exposed to the ICA culture and its supposed importance.

Everyone in the home office agreed that if a new president was to be named, it should be someone from within ICA. The question was who. Henry made it clear in his private meeting with Dick that it would be a difficult task. Dick and Dena wanted to make the choice easier for Henry. Board members would begin to whisper Dick's name into Henry's ear. It made perfect logic. The company needed someone from within to ensure continuity. It seemed obvious that no one was groomed or ready to assume the position at this time. Dick Washington was ready, and he had the executive experience. He understood finance and economics and had been on ICA's board for almost eleven years. He knew the company and had been hand picked by Henry Rothblatt for his present assignment.

Once he became president, Dick and Dena reasoned they could then begin Dick's ascension to the chairmanship of ICA's board. Members of the board knew that their vote for Richard Washington to become president of ICA would simultaneously be a vote for the eventual demutualization of ICA. Their vote would in turn disenfranchise all of ICA's policyholders while providing an opportunity for enormous wealth and an extraordinary windfall for whomever

Washington included in his plan, which meant each of them. Properly executed, the takeover of the company could be completed within the next six months. Taking the company public, they knew, would take a bit longer.

While Dick and Dena began plotting and executing their strategy, David was meeting with the executive committee. He brought them up to date on everything, sharing with them the details of his meeting with Washington at the Wrigley Building Grill. Others in the group reported similar experiences. Except for one dissenter, they agreed that Dick Washington had only his own self-interest in mind and that he was capable of devastating ICA if given the authority to do so. The lone dissenter was Jerry Barton, vice president in charge of mass marketing, or group sales, at it was technically known within ICA.

"I think you're all being a little too hard on Washington; he's new to the role and probably a little unsure of himself. He may be coming on a little strong but that's probably to let everyone know who's boss. If you look at the man's record it's hard to argue with; he's been very successful at everything he's undertaken. At the very least, I think we owe him a little more time." David made a mental note to find out if Barton had as yet had his meeting with Washington. He thought it might also be a good idea if he and Jerry met and discussed such a meeting, if it had taken place.

"Jerry may have a point," said Tim Walker. "Dick is Henry's appointment. Who the hell is going to tell Henry how he's behaving?"

"No one just yet," David interjected. "I'm working on a few things I want to get taken care of first. If we go to Henry we better be fully armed and sure of our position. What we have to do is begin thinking about who to propose to Henry as president of this company. Anyone Washington recommends will already be in his pocket and that would probably mean the end of ICA as we know it. Anyone have a thought or idea?"

There was silence. Each man had thought of people but just as Henry had done, they were mentally discarded as lacking in one area or another. Bob Wellington's name was floated, but he felt he was too old to get a positive board reaction. Tim's name was mentioned, and he felt compelled to tell them all of his conversation with Henry after the last executive committee meeting. They were still at square one, stuck in the mud without four wheel drive.

"Corey."

"What?" asked Bob Wellington.

"Corey, Corey Topping." It was Tim who had spoken.

Daryl Green said softly, "He's awfully young and inexperienced. What makes you feel he'd be a good candidate?"

"Well he's young looking, but actually he's a few years older than David, and as my closest assistant, I've worked with him in actuarial for nearly twenty years. He's bright, articulate, and has a photographic memory. A description of him as a brilliant thinker isn't an overstatement."

"Corey also worked directly for Henry during Tim's illness," chipped in Wellington. "I can tell you Henry spoke very highly of him."

"He's always been easy for me to work with," said David.

"What about investment experience?" asked Daryl.

Jerry Barton spoke. "Look, I don't know about this; you're talking about a guy who at the present time is only a second vice president of this company. I'm sure Corey is a very competent actuary, Tim, but no one knows better than you, there is a huge difference between being a very good actuary and having the ability to run ICA on a day-in and day-out basis. Why he's never…"

Before Jerry Barton could finish his sentence, a new voice was heard. Joe Swallow, a very quiet individual who seldom spoke up at executive committee meetings. "I know I usually don't contribute much at these meetings; primarily because we take up topics of little interest to my area, investments. But I happen to know a little bit about Corey, and I can tell you he's one very bright guy. We've played some tennis together, and while we work in different areas of the company, we've served together on several committees. If you'd like me to, I'd be happy to visit with him and find out the depth of his understanding about the kind of specialized investing we do here. I can report back to you within a matter of a couple of days."

"David, you haven't said much," Bob Wellington said.

"I like Corey. I'm just trying to anticipate in my mind how the board or Henry, for that matter, would react to our proposal that a forty-year-old second vice president can run this company. But, he's got one major advantage: Corey knows the company, he understands what we're about."

"Well, I just want to go on record as saying that I can't endorse Corey Topping for president of ICA." Jerry Barton stood. He slowly began to walk toward the windows of the conference room they were using and looked down at the small dots representing traffic and people on Michigan Avenue. "I just think Topping is too inexperienced. There must be a better choice."

David began to get an uncomfortable feeling from the tone of Barton's remarks. He again thought that it was important he meet with Jerry to discuss any contact he may have had with Dick Washington.

Before Barton could continue, Bob Wellington stood and walked over to the window next to Barton; he put his arm on his shoulder and turned to the rest of the group as he said, "Look, we haven't agreed to endorse Corey at this point, only to investigate the possibility. Until we come up with a better solution, if there is one, I suggest we look into this. Joe, you get us together a.s.a.p. after talking with Corey."

"You've got it," replied Swallow.

"There is one more thing," said David, stopping them in their tracks as they had risen to leave the room. "First, none of this leaves this room. Joe, I don't think you should let Corey know much at this point, keep it low key, casual. Also, Tim, you and I should present this to Henry when the time is right. He's home now and we can see him there. We've also got to clue him in to what's going on with Washington. Bob, I'd like you to visit with Boris and make certain none of this leaks to newspapers or rating agencies. We've got to keep the lid on tight."

As each man nodded his head in agreement they broke up. Tim stood alongside David. "You're sure we all know what the hell we're getting into?"

David looked at Tim and where David saw a degree of uncertainty, Tim looking into David's face saw only confidence. "I think so, but the way I see it, ICA's board will soon be asked to approve a new president. They don't know it yet, but they'll probably be voting on demutualization through the candidate they decide to appoint. If Washington's candidate wins, this company will never be the same."

A short while later David left the building and hailed a cab. As he rode along toward Lincoln Park on the way to his apartment he was debating what to do for dinner. Take in? Eat out? Pizza, chicken? Then he reached into his briefcase and pulled out his cellular and dialed Lisa's number. What he got was her answering machine again. When he had left a message yesterday her machine mentioned she would be out on a trip overnight but would be back late this afternoon. He thought about leaving another message but decided it would not be cool to appear anxious. David hung up.

Further to the north of where David lived and closer to the lake on Marine Drive, Joe Swallow was washing up before his wife put dinner on the table. As he looked at his face in the mirror, he thought to himself that if Henry Rothblatt wanted Corey Topping as the new president of ICA then so would he. Whatever Henry wanted, he would get if Joe Swallow had anything to say about it.

Joe was a recovering alcoholic. After graduating from a Jesuit school and two years in their seminary, Joe decided the priesthood was not what he wanted. Although he had appeared to adjust to a secular life quite well after five years of marriage and two children, Joe's guilt over having left the seminary caught up with him. They say most alcoholics have it in their genes. Maybe, but Joe knew of no one in his family who had a similar problem. But then, no one in his family had deserted his God.

By the time Joe had joined ICA and ascended to the top of the Investment Department, he was a sneak drinker of immense proportions. He had a unique ability to begin drinking after work, and keep belting down the Jack Daniels and sodas until one or two in the morning, yet still show up at his office at 8 A.M. looking, and apparently feeling, ready for a good day's work.

His wife nagged him about his habit but he denied it. Minor traffic accidents occurred while he was intoxicated and he denied it.

One evening after slamming his car into a fence on a bridge that spanned a small creek, while on vacation, and breaking an arm and a rib, he could no longer deny it. He was ticketed for driving under the influence and lost his privilege to drive for one year. Worst of all, Henry got wind of Joe's troubles. Joe was summoned to Henry's office after he had returned to work. He expected the worst.

Joe recalled that meeting vividly and as he did a small, warm smile came to his face. Henry was solicitous of his well-being and asked if he was still drinking. Joe was an alcoholic, but an honest one. "Yes," he had told Henry. "I've got a major problem—don't know that I can ever stop."

"Well, Joe, you're going to have to stop or lose your position here at ICA." Joe heard nothing he had not expected up to that point. "But we're not there yet, Joe, not yet. I've made a few inquiries and a few calls. This is the name, address, and phone number of the best alcohol recovery center in this area. They're expecting you to check in before 5 P.M. They'll help you get started on recovery. Of course, it's really all up to you. If you check in and complete the program, and, of course, as long as you never take another drink, you can return to work when you're ready, and we'll welcome you with open arms."

Joe was astonished that Henry had put this all together, but before he could say anything, or thank Henry, he heard more from the boss. "Joe, take one more drink, make even one slip-up, and your ass is out of here. Do you understand? Joe, do you understand me?"

Joe Swallow, tears in his eyes, nodded affirmatively. He never slipped, he never again had a drink, and he found another god, Henry Rothblatt. Henry wants Corey Topping, he'll get him if Joe had anything to say about it.

CHAPTER 20

Mike Spellari was becoming frustrated. At home, Marie, his wife, noticed his agitation. Mike sloughed it off, but his mood was unmistakable. The frustration he felt was due to the wall he kept running into whenever he pursued information on Dick Washington. He could get just so far and no farther before hitting a dead end. The facts surrounding his retirement from Batem Electronics were particularly difficult to come by.

While Mike contemplated his next move, Marie yelled out that he had a phone call. It was David, who proceeded to bring him up to date on the executive committee meeting of that morning. The updating started with a detailed description of his breakfast with Washington. He filled Mike in on the Corey Topping issue, and Mike's response was "not a bad idea."

Mike told David of his inability to get any additional substantive information on their nemesis, Mr. Washington. "But I've got an idea." David was all ears. "Look, I know it could be dangerous, but we need professional help. Let's hire a private investigator. I know a guy that can do this; he's good and he's discreet."

David interrupted, "He would have to be. For God's sake, can you imagine if anyone found out the company was investigating its own officer, temporary or not?"

"David, I don't think the company should hire this guy. You and the company can't be connected to this. I want to call John, Jerry, Dave, and a couple of other G.A.'s. We all ought to be willing to participate in this deal and we can foot the bill for the PI. That keeps it out of corporate. The seven of us have as much or more to lose than anybody else. We've got lots of time and business invested with ICA."

"Mike, I really want to keep this among as few people as possible. You know how the grapevine works; if we let field people in on this, it could really spread."

"I'm in on it," snapped Mike. "I haven't told anyone."

"I'm sorry, Mike, I know that, but you can understand my concern."

"David, we've got to get the scoop on this guy. Let's call these guys and explain what's going on. I'll guarantee that no one will let a word of this leak to anyone."

"Maybe you're right," David heard himself say. The words surprised him. "But you get your guy to do the investigation and I'll talk with the other six guys. I've got to make them understand how important it is to keep this situation out of the press. I'll talk with each of them by noon tomorrow. You call them after that and make whatever financial arrangements you want to. You're right, we've got to keep ICA out of that end of things."

David mentioned that Tim Walker and he were planning to visit Henry at home and fill him in on what was going on. He said he was concerned about getting Henry to believe his friend Washington was really a Jew-hating bastard who had only his own self-interest at heart and was ready to tear ICA apart at the seams. Mike thought to himself that David and Tim had a tough job in store. Henry prided himself on his knowledge of people. It wouldn't be easy for him to admit he might have made a serious mistake in judgment about Washington.

David also shared his suspicions regarding Jerry Barton.

"Another son of a bitch," Mike said. "You know, I've never liked that guy. Can't tell you why; there's just something about him that doesn't sit right with me. I don't know; he's just one cold fish."

"Well, I'm going to try to get to him and find out if he and Washington have had any dealings." The two men agreed to stay in close touch.

Mike picked up the phone once more. This time he dialed and when a voice answered he said, "Morty, it's Mike Spellari; I need to see you." Morty was a private detective, sort of. Arrangements were made for them to meet at a west side coffee shop at eight o'clock the following morning.

Back at his office David looked at the stack of calls he needed to return. Thank God for Meredith, his secretary, and several great regional directors he could depend on. He would spread the calls to them; his mind just wasn't on his normal work load. All David could think about, as he leaned back in his chair and looked out at the lake over the tops of several buildings, was how he and Tim would present this to Henry. He was certain Henry's reaction would be one of incredulity. It was, after all, an incredulous situation.

CHAPTER 21

Henry sat in a very old wicker rocking chair, his screened porch overlooking the Ravines on one side of the house and Lake Michigan on the other. This house was one of the few real luxuries that he had allowed into his life, in spite of his wealth. Many thought Henry to be much wealthier than he actually was. No one needed to run a tag day for ICA's president and chairman but neither did his annual income stack up with others in the business world with similar responsibilities. As a mutual company there were no stock options, only annual bonuses which were not of the humongous variety. He had a very generous pension and profit-sharing plan as did all of ICA's employees. His salary was in the high six figures, but well under the seven figures so common among industry leaders.

Most of Henry's personal wealth came from living a conservative lifestyle. He and Ruth saved and invested wisely. Their home was one of the few things Henry allowed them that was the least bit ostentatious.

The Ravines are a small area in Highland Park near the lake. They roll and pitch and are filled in the spring and summer with green-leafed trees and vegetation. Deer live in the woods and frequently can be seen and admired for their rich beauty. Henry loved his thirty-year-old, two-story home. He especially enjoyed the porch in the spring, and early fall. He could sit and read for hours, and his heaven on earth was complete whenever Ruth joined him. Symphonic music drifted softly from inside the house onto his beloved porch and out into the woods. It was serene and he was at home and comfortable.

The doorbell rang and Ruth moved from the kitchen toward the front door. "I'll get it, dear. It must be David and Tim."

They were received by Henry in his rocking chair; he motioned them to a sofa and placed his legs upon the ottoman. Ruth offered them tea or coffee; neither man wanted anything so she retired to her kitchen. Henry adored her chicken matzo ball soup, and she loved to make it for him. David thought Henry looked even better than when he had seen him a few days earlier at the hospital. "You're looking pretty good Chief."

"Well, I'm at least feeling human again, although I've got a few sores inside my mouth." Tim and David shot each other a glance. Both men were aware that with very high levels of chemotherapy it would not be unusual for ulcers to appear as a side effect. Unfortunately, they could form in the mouth and throat. Henry probably knew that too. It could be a monstrous problem if it occurred.

David got right to it. "Henry, we've got a problem." After twenty minutes or so of bringing the stone-faced executive up to date, including both his breakfast meeting with Washington and the executive committee meeting, David paused. Tim sat by, not having, as yet, said much.

Before either could proceed, Henry interrupted, "What do either of you think we should do about this situation? You've mentioned the executive committee's suggestion of Corey Topping; anything else?"

Tim and David were stunned. They had expected at least surprise from Henry, but all Henry wanted to know was where do they go from here?

"Henry, aren't you a little surprised by this?" asked Tim.

"A bit disturbed?" questioned David.

"Well, I am disturbed, of course. How can you know someone for this long and yet not really know him? Surprised, no. Fifteen minutes after Mr. Washington had lunch with one of the board, Kevin McDougal, I was on the phone with Kevin. He called to tell me that he had been invited to lunch by Dick and that although somewhat subtle in his approach, Richard had left no doubt in Kevin's mind that control of ICA is what he had in mind. It didn't take much of an effort on either of our parts to figure out that the control of a mutual life insurance company is not worth the time and effort our friend Mr. Washington seems to be giving it, unless he had it in mind also to demutalize ICA and take it public. All of this, of course, would be after he made certain that he was appropriately rewarded by the company for doing so."

Tim and David were dumbfounded. Henry, with a little help from a friend on the board, had it all figured out. "I'm not happy, of course. I'm plenty surprised, disappointed really, in my judgment of Dick Washington. What we have to do, however, is figure out where we stand. Has Washington won any board members over yet? If so, how many has he persuaded to see things his way?"

David had not yet told Henry about his and Mike's plan to hire a private investigator to dig up whatever he could on Washington. Something told David, at least for the moment, to keep it to himself. Neither Tim or anyone else on the executive board knew anything about an investigator at this point.

"As for your committee's suggestion for me to name Corey Topping as president of ICA, well, let's just say that at this time, while I don't exclude the possibility, it's a bit premature and very radical. A presidential candidate still has to be someone I can sell to the board."

"I realize you're both a bit surprised at what I already know, but let me give you another bit of a shock. Dena Callahan, whom I named to her first major board, is taking sides with Washington, so we know there are at least two board members lost to us. David, I'll need you, Tim, and perhaps Bob Wellington to arrange your own informal lunches, dinners, or whatever to get our side of the story out. You need to keep me informed regularly with any move Dick might make. Now, if you'll excuse me, I'm a bit tired."

As David and Tim stood to leave, David didn't like what Henry now looked like. In just the hour since they had arrived Henry had paled badly and looked weakened. He hoped it was his imagination. Before leaving, David stopped in the kitchen, put his arm around Ruth and gave her a hug. "If there's anything you need...," Ruth took his face in her hands. As she looked at David with a faint smile, he saw her eyes were slightly red and damp. They hugged and held each other for a moment. David returned to the porch to say goodbye to Henry but he had already left, headed for his bedroom.

David and Tim drove back downtown, going the long way through Evanston and the North Shore, past both Northwestern and Loyola Universities. After the usual traffic, they entered Lake Shore Drive. Little had been said, and David finally whispered, "I don't know, Tim, I don't know."

CHAPTER 22

A few days after his visit with David and Tim, Henry was rushed back into Rush Presbyterian Hospital. The chemo was playing havoc with his immune system. Blister-like sores had broken out in his mouth and continued down into his throat. Trying to drink or eat was excruciating. Even swallowing air was painful. The doctors did a few tests and explained to Ruth that she was witnessing, not the ravages of the cancer, but rather of the treatment.

Drugs could help alleviate his pain, but the sores would have to run their course. The doctors would do what they could to keep him comfortable but the only way to avoid discomfort and severe pain would be to give him drugs and sedatives that would keep him asleep, in a coma-like state. At this point anyway, Henry did not want that. He needed to think. He needed his wits about him, pain or not. For the next several days the gritty warrior dealt with almost unbearable pain, but deal with it he did.

CHAPTER 23

Dick Washington sat with Barry Hornsfelt; they were having dinner at The Tavern on Rush. Tavern was a steak and Italian restaurant that, since its opening, had become one of Rush Street's hottest eateries. Downstairs was a huge bar catering to a sea of single people in their early thirties to late forties. The bar was busy, swinging and loud.

Up a flight of stairs was the restaurant, small, with windows overlooking Rush Street. It had become a hangout for Chicago's politicians, lawyers, and other upscale professionals and businessmen. The food was good and huge portions filled plates everywhere. Dick Washington liked it along with the added advantage of its being within walking distance of his residence on State Parkway.

Barry Hornsfelt was president of LBS, Lincoln Banking Systems, a group of mid-sized banks. He was also the bank's largest stockholder and chairman of their board. Henry and Barry had both come to Chicago at about the same time many years earlier. Henry was a young graduate actuary taking his first job out of college with ICA. Barry was going into banking with one of LBS's many predecessors. They met on a double date and became good friends. Both married the women they dated that night. Over the years Barry and his wife often played bridge with Henry and Ruth, and they frequently traveled together.

Dick knew Barry from their service as ICA board members. Barry had been on the board a few years longer than Dick. After the waiter took their drink orders, Dick, a martini, Barry, a light beer, Dick looked right into Barry's eyes with a soulful look on his face and said, "I guess you've heard the bad news about Henry."

"Yes, yes I have, it's too bad."

"You know, Barry, as two of ICA's senior board members I wanted to suggest that it's up to you and me to make certain that ICA stays on track during Henry's illness."

"Why shouldn't it?" asked Barry, innocently.

"Well, it could be quite some time until Henry returns, assuming

71

he does return. I'm already feeling a certain combination of uneasiness and tension around the company."

"Really, from whom?" asked Barry.

"Well, just the rank and file, though even a few of the management team seem a bit unsettled."

"Dick, I sense you have something additional on your mind; I'd really like to know what it is."

"What makes you think that?" inquired Washington.

"You and I have known each other for ten years. In all of that time we've never met outside of a board function. Suddenly you call me for dinner; I suppose you could say I just have a suspicious nature."

A slight fake chuckle escaped from Dick's lips. "Never underestimate a banker," he said. "Okay, since you ask, I believe the board should have a strong hand in the appointment of a new president. Henry is sixty-eight years old and at best can serve as COB for two more years. When he's seventy, the company mandates retirement. I view the presidency as a more immediate concern since at ICA the president is also the chief executive officer. I just don't think Henry will ever again be strong enough to fill those roles. Believe me, no one has more respect for Henry's accomplishments at ICA than I do. Of course I hesitate to point out that had Henry created a workable succession plan, the company wouldn't presently be in the position it finds itself. However, I really think the matter demands our immediate attention."

Washington was not aware that Barry had called Bob Wellington prior to his dinner with Dick. Nor was he aware that Bob had brought Barry up to speed on what seemed to be happening, and he was most certainly not aware that Wellington had given him an interesting piece of information and that the two men had discussed how Barry could use it.

"Dick, how old are you?"

"Fifty-five," Washington had answered. "Why do you ask?"

"Well, it's just that it seems such a young age to retire; I'm envious of you. I've got to wait for at least another year. I'll probably go longer, though. Say, you know, it might pay for me to mention something to you. Are you aware of the ICA rules governing board membership?"

"What rules are you taking about?" Dick asked cautiously.

"Well, for instance, are you aware the board requires a member to hold a title of president, or the equivalent, in a company similar in stature to ICA? In the event that a director loses that position he or she has eighteen months in which to be appointed to a new position of title. If a director fails to do so, he's automatically unseated. Tell me, Dick, when did you officially retire from Batem Electronics?"

Washington was vaguely aware of the rule Barry had just mentioned but he had somehow never connected it to himself. He thought for a moment and then, "I retired fourteen months ago."

"Do you think you'll be repositioned in the next couple of months? I'd hate to think of losing you." By this time the waiter had placed their drinks and menus in front of them. He would return in a few minutes for their orders. Barry lifted his glass of beer and smiled behind it as he took a drink. Dick stared at his martini as he turned it around in his hand by the stem of the glass.

"Well, my situation will resolve itself, I think." That was the best Washington could offer. Through the rest of their dinner he could not bring himself to get back to his original reason for the meeting. There was some general conversation and little of that. Barry thanked Dick for dinner, the two men shook hands and went their separate ways.

As Washington walked back toward his home he was horrified that he had not given more thought to the board rule Barry had pointed out to him. He decided that it just meant he would have to have himself appointed as president and COB before the end of the year. December 31st, it all had to be done by then. This was good, he thought. Now he had a deadline. It gave him more purpose and his adrenaline began to flow. Never mind that clearly Barry Hornsfelt was clearly not in his camp. He needed Dena. He needed to feel her; he needed to suck up her strength to get recharged. He stopped at a corner pay phone and placed a call.

CHAPTER 24

Nancy Wagner sat in the small kitchen of her condominium, located in what is known as the DePaul area. The neighborhood had a distinctively yuppie feel to it though Nancy felt far from that. Over the past ten years the neighborhood around DePaul University had been transformed from that of a typical middle-class Chicago neighborhood to a completely renovated, sophisticated and smart upper middle class setting. The building was completely new from the ground up and consisted of, from the outside, what looked to be town homes. In reality however, they were condo apartments with a fence running the length of the block and electronic gated doors that opened into a well-landscaped courtyard.

It was Saturday afternoon and she was in her robe. Although she had awakened around 6:00 A.M., as usual, she had no real plans for the day, or the weekend for that matter. She couldn't fall back to sleep. She had gone to bed around two o'clock in the morning but was kept awake both last night and this morning by an assortment of thoughts that kept running through her mind. Ordinarily, she was a very clear thinker and well organized, but for the past few days, her mind had been muddled and confused. Over and over again she thought about her years with Henry, how wonderful they had been. She thought about how Henry and ICA had been her family and provided her with stability and opportunity.

A plain-looking woman with few close personal friends, Nancy had almost no family. Her mother and father had both died within a year of each other when she was only eleven. After their deaths, an aunt and uncle who owned a farm in western Illinois near Galena had raised her. While she was attending secretarial school in Peoria her aunt and uncle were killed in a car accident. They left the farm to her, having no children of their own. When Nancy received the news of their tragic deaths she had been away at school, and though she inherited the farm, she had never returned to it after her aunt's and uncle's funeral. Arrangements were made for its sale and the small amount left after paying off the mortgage and other debts was used to pay the balance of her housing and tuition.

At nineteen, Nancy graduated from Mrs. Geary's Secretarial School and secured a position with Caterpillar Company in Peoria. After working there for almost two years, she decided Chicago would offer far more in the way of cultural activities and an ability to build a life for herself. She asked for and received a transfer to Caterpillar's Chicago office. After just a few months she saw an ad for secretaries at ICA and decided a change to a new business environment couldn't hurt. She felt, in retrospect, it was the best decision of her life.

By her twenty-fifth birthday, Nancy Wagner had worked herself up ICA's employment ladder and into the position of secretary to Henry Rothblatt, the then new president of ICA. She was proud of herself and vowed to be the best secretary any corporate leader could possibly want. She had succeeded eminently. Nancy had now served over fifteen years for Henry, and their relationship was part mentor to student, part father to child, part friend to friend.

But her social life never got off the ground. Between long hours at ICA and her shyness and lack of sophistication, Nancy had not had an easy time of it. While she had many nice acquaintances at ICA, she had few close friends at work. Mostly, she shuffled between her small condo and the office. She found Mondays to be especially difficult; she was forced to respond to polite questions about her weekend and often found herself making up white lies about how they were spent. In reality, she usually took in a movie or walked to the zoo with another woman, older than she, in her building. They had met in the building's commissary while grocery shopping. The older woman, a widow, was more outgoing than Nancy and would urge her to get out more. But Nancy's life simply went on the same day after day.

At work she was happiest, and whenever Henry in a relaxed moment spent time with her and chatted she was in heaven. She was especially intrigued by his stories of travel all over the world. Nancy had the money to do as much traveling as she wanted to. Her salary as Henry Rothblatt's secretary had grown handsomely. Her future was secure. She had a wonderful pension and profit-sharing program of which all ICA employees were a part. Because of her seniority, she had even worked her way up to four weeks vacation annually. She had never taken more than two weeks in a year.

In addition to her investment in the condo, she conservatively invested all the rest of her earnings. On several occasions, Henry urged her to take advantage of her personal situation. He made untold suggestions for travel. But other than a trip to New York that he had given to her on her fortieth birthday, she had not left Chicago. She was terrified in New York. Henry had given her a ticket to a Broadway play but because she was uncertain of her surroundings, she didn't use it. She couldn't wait to get back to Chicago and things that were familiar.

As unsure of herself as Nancy was with outsiders and unfamiliar territories, so sure was she at the office. Henry's business schedule was run, due to her efforts, with absolute precision. He never had to attend to a detail, travel plans, mail, telephone, or appointments—all were watched over carefully by his talented secretary. Her efforts were totally appreciated and Henry went out of his way to reward her and include her in his world, whenever the opportunity arose. She had been in the Rothblatt home on many occasions and was also a part of many company affairs, always in the background but always ready to do whatever Henry required of her.

It had been difficult to watch Mr. Richard Washington move into Henry's office, even if only temporarily. She accepted her assignment to serve as his secretary until Henry's return, and she had looked at Washington as a friend of Henry's, someone here to help ICA through this period of what she hoped would be Henry's recuperation.

Everything had been fine the first several days though she noticed Mr. Washington's style was very different from Henry's. She was used to a calm demeanor around the presidential office; now she found a demeanor that was both pompous and coarse. Henry never swore, Washington seldom did not. Nevertheless, she felt good about being able to answer Washington's questions and had reason to believe she could be of genuine help to him. A few days after the arrangement began, things began to change. There was all this talk of importance of profits and the lack of necessity for company culture. And then there was the morning Washington had come into the office after a breakfast meeting with David Rourke.

Nancy was really very fond of David. She was of course biased towards him because she knew Henry thought so much of the young man. Henry had once commented, "His parents should be very proud of that young man. I'd be proud if he were my boy."

But here was Mr. Washington ranting and raving about David Rourke as if he were a criminal. "Son of a bitch" was heard more than once. She could not have imagined what might have occurred at their meeting.

During the past few weeks other meetings had taken place. Many with Jerry Barton. She knew Jerry and was somewhat indifferent to him. Henry thought Barton was good at his job but he never commented personally about him the way he had so many times about David.

There were a number of meetings Nancy had set up for Washington with board members. All of the meetings took place one-on-one. Dena Callahan called Mr. Washington several times each week. Recently Washington had requested airline tickets to New York and hotel reservations for him and Ms. Callahan in both New York and Atlantic City. Supposedly they were to meet with a group of bankers. What kind of meeting took place with a bank, over a weekend, she wondered.

Nancy poured herself another cup of coffee and walked to the bedroom. She should get dressed and get out for a walk but she sat on the edge of her bed, coffee cup in hand, and thought about the memos. Did anyone else know what they were planning, she wondered? She had been thinking about this for several days and debating if she should mention them to Henry. But he must know, she thought. So many strange things were happening.

Nancy ruled out talking to Henry about the memos she had typed, out of respect for his privacy and the rest he needed at this time. Who else could she talk to? David Rourke, of course, but would she be considered disloyal for telling him of confidential memos to which he was not a party? She just didn't know what the right move was. She thought about it but was confused and uncertain.

77

PART II
SEPTEMBER – NOVEMBER 1996

CHAPTER 25

The Oak Street Beach, alive with sunbathers, swimmers, and ball-throwing, sand-kicking kids during July and August, becomes relatively calm after Labor Day. Chicago was still sunny but already there was a noticeable dip in the temperature. The public schools had opened and the after summer traffic increased in its intensity as vacationers headed back to their jobs. The leaves on the trees would soon begin to turn into their autumn hues

At the ICA Building everything appeared perfectly normal. The elevators were running precisely and monotonously on time, carrying passengers to and from their same old floors. The granite and marble foyer still captured an occasional gasp from new visitors as they took in artwork, sculptures, and the breathtaking beauty as the light from outside played over the contemporary, even modernistic, interior. The top thirty floors of the eighty-floor structure also seemed perfectly normal. The mail boys made their rounds, office workers carried their coffee from canteen to desk, the conversations, the flirting, all seemed as it should be. But this was not a true picture of what was actually taking place, and as David sat, slouched, really, on his office couch at the end of a long week, he recapped in his mind where it all stood.

Henry had completed his chemotherapy treatments and after a short rest was about to begin radiation in a further effort to eradicate the cancer or at least to slow its progress. While he had not come into the office, he had visited with David, Tim, and Mike at home. He seemed okay, though he had lost considerable weight and had a somewhat grayish pallor about him. Nevertheless, he was now actively involved in the strategy to elect the next president of the company and was planning to return as ICA's chairman. David hoped that this was not too optimistic an outlook. He understood that, although Henry might resume his duties as chairman, the board would still be free to follow Dick Washington's lead should they choose. Washington would put up a candidate for president of ICA to oppose whomever Henry might come up with. Should he win, it would mean that Washington would be in a position to press for demutalization and to take ICA public. It was all a question of selling the board and harvesting the votes. Certainly the struggle for control would be a bit easier with Henry actively at the helm.

His physicians had told Henry he could return to work when he felt ready, and he had told David that, while he felt comparatively well now, his endurance would be severely challenged while undergoing radiation and even afterward. David thought that anything would be better than chemotherapy. Thank God the episode with the blisters had subsided. David thought about how brave Henry had been and wondered if he could have withstood all that Henry was enduring, exacerbated by the mental strain.

For the past few weeks selected members of the executive committee had been meeting discreetly at Henry's home in the late afternoon. While he had not made known his personal choice to assume ICA's presidency, he had discussed several possibilities with them including, Corey Topping. Noticeably absent from their meetings was Jerry Barton. Henry, though somewhat reluctantly, had come to the same conclusion as David and the others. Barton was a snake in the grass. Washington had apparently persuaded Barton that the two of them could steer the ICA ship and Barton was enthusiastic about accepting Richard Washington as his leader if it meant a monumental move up the ladder to the president's office at ICA.

Tim, David, and Bob Wellington were convinced that Jerry had been passing the meat of their executive committee meetings back to Washington, and thus his exclusion from their recent sessions. They continued to hold their regular Friday morning meetings with Barton present but kept the agenda to matters other than succession issues.

As for Washington, recently he had become somewhat unstable holding frequent, impromptu meetings with department heads and other employees and staff.

As David thought about the events of the past few months, he recalled the single most important thing that had occurred if they were to keep Richard Washington from stealing the company. David closed his eyes and traces of a smile appeared on his face as he recalled the phone call he had received from Mike.

As David reviewed the event in his mind, he remembered the

usual Heinie in his hand as he sat in boxer shorts, feet outstretched in front of his TV. He loved reruns of the <u>Honeymooners.</u> In the episode he was watching Norton was teaching Ralph to play golf. Jackie Gleason was hysterical, but to David, Art Carney was the show. This was the famous "Hello Ball" episode and David was laughing out loud. Upstairs he heard more laughter and wondered if the college kids were up there watching the same show. He remembered thinking that the humor spanned generations.

Earlier in the day he had placed yet another call to Lisa and once more talked with her answering machine. He was confounded by the number of times they had tried to reach each other without success. He hoped it wasn't some kind of a sign, that in spite of their best efforts, for one screwy reason after another, they had not talked directly to each other much less actually gotten together. He left a message for her to call him, and he let her know he would be home all night. She was supposed to return from a three-day segment and he hoped she would make it back in time to return his call tonight.

Lisa always sounded wonderful when she left messages and she encouraged David to keep trying to reach her. He wondered, if she saw him now, if she would keep encouraging him. His shorts and a filthy, food-stained sweatshirt covered him, and with a can of beer in his hand he didn't exactly look like a poster boy for the YMCA. Lisa, he thought, would be horrified. The cold pizza and the smell of an apartment that needed a good cleaning would not, he mused, help the situation.

Breaking into hysterical laughter coming from the TV, the telephone sounded and he immediately let out an involuntary "Thank you, God" and pumped his fist, "Yes!" He let it ring a couple of times before he picked it up fully expecting to hear Lisa's voice.

"Mr. Rourke, I presume." It was not Lisa, but he knew the voice.

"No, Mike, it's Desi Arnaz. What do you want? Lucille and I are working a charity event."

"Well, at least you're with a woman, even if she has been dead for several years."

"Yeah, but she's still funnier than you. What's going on?"

"Buddy, I think we've hit the jack pot, and I'm not talking Bingo;

we've just won the lottery."

"What the hell are you talking about? Come on Mike, make sense. I want to see the end of the Honeymooners."

"Well, my man, what I've got just might send you to the moon. I received our private detective's report."

"And?"

"And, it turns out our friend Mr. Washington did not exactly retire from Batem Electronics. It seems he was fired."

"Okay, well that's something. What did he do, steal a laptop?"

"Probably, but that's not the big news. It seems Dicky boy got a little too friendly with his secretary; the problem is, she was a twenty-three-year-old young lady who didn't appreciate his attention. After several months of fighting him off, she filed a sexual harassment suit against him and Batem. To keep things quiet and out of court she was handed a nice sum of cash and Dick was handed his walking papers." There was a pause as Mike gloated. David thought through the situation for a moment.

"You know, Mike, I was waiting for a call from Lisa. I can't believe I'm saying this, but I'm glad it was you."

CHAPTER 26

Dena luxuriated in the bath of her South Shore apartment. The richly appointed two-bedroom apartment was located close to the university; she could see the lake with an unobstructed view. As the telephone sounded she was tempted not to answer. She was relaxing in the warmth of the tub while its jets gently whirled the scented water around her. She alternated her thinking between how she and Dick would pull off their takeover of ICA and what she would do with the resulting windfall. She picked up the cordless phone at the side of tub.

"Hello."

"Dena? It's Dick. I'm on my way to see Henry; I just wanted to touch base."

"Why not come over and touch me?" She smiled to herself. She knew just how to play the silly, rich old fart. "I'm taking a bath at the moment and the only thing I'm wearing is my nail polish."

"That's a very tempting offer. How about getting together for a late dinner when I finish at Henry's?"

"Sounds yummy, but I really thought I'd just get into bed early tonight and read. I'm really way behind and I'm also very tired. What about a raincheck until later this week?"

"Later this week? Dena, I want to see you tonight. Come on, Dena."

She could hear the urgency in his voice. The silly bastard is going to cry she thought. Well, too bad. Let him stew for a day or so. "Honestly, Dick, I'm exhausted."

"Come on, Dena, come on, please."

His desperation amused her. "I can't, sweetie, not tonight. Call me tomorrow at my office after nine, tell me about your meeting tonight, and maybe we can get together. Good night, pussycat." She placed the phone back in its cradle and ended the call.

Serves him right, she thought, let him stifle his horny little dick for one night. After all, she wasn't his private sperm receptacle. Careful, she reminded herself, she couldn't afford to get too nasty with him, not just yet. He still led the assault on ICA, and she wanted to be a beneficiary of the result. With the couple of million she estimated as her profit when they took ICA public, she would have an excellent start for the secure life she so urgently wanted and needed. No more screwing men like Dick Washington in order to get ahead. Her job paid her handsomely but not enough to allow her to invest on a big time basis. She knew if she had the money to put into the market, she could make it big; with her brains and looks, the combination could be deadly. She had the ability to extract information from people that she could use very advantageously. As head of the university's business school and with her femininity, she could make a fortune. She just needed the capital to get started.

She would drive Washington mad with desire but in the end she'd give him what he wanted...her. Damn, she thought, she really wanted to know what Dick and Henry would be discussing at their meeting. Maybe she should have agreed to that late dinner.

Needing to relax, Dena closed her eyes, leaned back, and slowly sank deeper into the tub. She raised one leg in the air and watched the water drip from her toes. She put her foot down; her hand reached for the faucet and turned it on. She arranged for the water to flow gently from the hand-held shower head, which she picked up. With the shower head held in her right hand, her left hand grazed gently over her breasts and touched her nipples. Slowly, she lowered the shower head between her outstretched legs. Her face tensed in pleasure and she thought momentarily that no man was really necessary. As she shuddered and then totally relaxed, she smiled. Well, maybe Richard Washington was necessary, but only for a short while.

CHAPTER 27

The doorbell rang and Henry lifted himself from his leather chair, laid aside his book and afghan, then walked slowly to the front door. He was expecting Dick Washington to stop by right about now; he had invited his acting chairman so they could discuss a number of matters. He opened the door and welcomed Washington into the foyer. They walked together, Henry leading the way back into the living room.

As Washington looked around the room that he had sat in on more than one occasion, he noticed little, if any, change since his last visit. Comfortably furnished, the room featured a large, presently unlit, fireplace. Perpendicular to the hearth were two couches with a coffee table in between. On the table were coffee books, one of which Washington noticed dealt with the Great Golf Courses of the World. A candy dish filled with brightly colored hard candies also sat on the table. Waterford, Dick thought to himself. Henry noticed him glancing at the candy dish and said, "Help yourself."

"No, thank you, but it's a beautiful dish. Waterford, isn't it?"

"I don't really know; you'd have to ask Ruth."

"Where is Ruth? Is she home?"

"She's at our daughter's house for dinner tonight."

As Washington further glanced around he decided to sit at the end of one couch closest to the fireplace. Henry had already positioned himself in an overstuffed chair at the other end of the couches, facing the fireplace. As he crossed his thin legs, Washington thought Henry looked frail, but Dick Washington did not underestimate this frail old-looking man in the tan cardigan.

"Well, Henry, it's been a few weeks since I've seen you and you're looking pretty good," Washington lied. Actually, Henry looked pale and gaunt, he thought. Maybe he would do us all a favor and just die.

"Well, actually I'm not feeling too bad at the moment. It varies from day to day. I'm not fooling myself, Dick, I'm not getting better and I know it, but I need to hang around awhile in order to take care of some unfinished business."

"Now, come on, Henry, you'll be fine. New drugs are being discovered all the time, you just have to hang in there and believe."

After a momentary silence, Henry spoke.

"Dick, do you remember the club's two-man match play championship two years ago?"

"Like I could forget it? Why, you old scoundrel, you single-handedly beat us." Dick thought it curious that Henry would call up this particular memory.

"How well do you remember the events of that day?"

"Like it was yesterday," Washington responded, as he processed the memory. "Harry and I had you and Jimmy down by four holes after nine."

"Yes, and Jimmy and I were both feeling pretty ragged. Remember, we asked for a rescheduling of the match because both of us had been under the weather with the summer flu. As I recall, you refused and wouldn't give us an extension. You made us play the match. If I also recall correctly, it was a sweltering, humid day and Jimmy lost his lunch on the fifth hole."

"Well, Henry, you know me, I'm just a competitive SOB and I was really geared up to win that tournament. It wasn't personal in any way, we were just looking for an edge."

"Do you recall what happened after we made the turn?"

"I'd rather not."

"You never knew, Dick, how sore Jimmy and I were at the two of you for making us play. When we made the turn, we stopped at the men's room and while you and Harry lit cigars and grabbed a beer in the halfway house, Jimmy and I took Pepto Bismol and crapped our brains out. Jimmy wanted to withdraw and forfeit. I told him to go ahead if he felt he had to but I was damned if I would concede. We both agreed to keep going. If we couldn't win, by God, we were going to make a match of it...screw how we felt."

"Well, you certainly kept your vow; as I recall, you fellows rallied and tied us up on the sixteenth hole."

"Yes, and then the infamous seventeenth hole."

"Infamous, why infamous, Henry?"

"I'll tell you in a minute. We were still tied on the eighteenth tee, remember?"

"Of course I do."

"Dick, I don't think I had hit a ball on the fairway on number eighteen all year; that tight fairway had eaten me up off the tee all summer. Jimmy hadn't fared much better. As my low handicapper, it shook me up when his tee shot went into the woods. He was lucky to find it. But when I stood on the tee and thought about what the two of you had put us through, I decided to—how did you put it a moment ago?—oh yes, to hang in there. I believed. I believed I would hit the ball smack into the center of the fairway, and damned if I didn't."

Dick Washington was watching Henry intently. He knew he was dumping his bucket over an old grievance, but he wasn't certain if he was making a further point. "You sure did, Henry, and what did I do but hit one out of bounds. There went the match. Damn, to this day it just burns me that I did that, but, you were the better man that day."

"Well, I did learn a lesson. What was I then, sixty-six years old? What I learned was to hang in there and believe. I have you to thank for that lesson."

"What's this business about the infamous seventeenth hole?"

"Oh, yes, that was when you hit your second shot into some hardpan just to the right of the green, remember?"

Washington's face flushed. "No, I can't say that I do, I mean it's been two years, Henry."

"Well, I'll remind you that you subtly pushed the ball forward, out of the hardpan and into the grass. You didn't think either of us was in a position to see you, and we weren't, but my caddie was; he saw you do it quite clearly."

Furious, Washington replied, "Why he's a lying little fucker if he says I did that. I did no such thing."

"I didn't confront you with it because I found it difficult to believe you would do such a thing. I figured even if you did, it didn't alter the outcome of the match. You were a good friend and I chose not to make an issue of it. Besides, I convinced myself the caddie might be mistaken."

"Of course he was!"

"Was he? Now, I'm not so certain."

"Henry, what's this all about? It isn't about golf, is it?"

Henry, now weakened by the energy he had put into the recounting of the story, looked at Dick Washington, leaned forward, and staring directly into his eyes, said, "No, it's not about golf; it's about life. It's about cheating; it's about friendship and, most of all, it's about hanging in there and believing."

"I don't understand," said a visibly shaken Richard Washington.

"You may be a cheat and a scoundrel, Dick, but you're not dumb. You understand perfectly, but just remember this, I'm going to hang in there and I do believe that I'll retain every last thing I've spent a lifetime building, and this time you're not a friend so I will respond to your transgression."

There was a momentary silence as each man assessed the best way to end their discussion. Washington rose and simply said, "Don't bother to show me out,"and left.

CHAPTER 28

Joe Swallow had met with Corey Topping and reported back to the executive committee that his judgment was very positive concerning Corey having the necessary basics insofar as institutional investing was concerned. In addition, due to the time Corey had spent with Henry on a few special projects, he had a remarkably good reading on ICA's investment philosophy. "More importantly," he remarked, "I'd be excited and pleased to have him lead ICA."

"That's just preposterous," said Jerry Barton, who sat at the conference table holding a rippling cup of coffee due, as David noted, to a slight tremor in his hand. "Absolutely preposterous! Do you all realize what you're contemplating? A second vice president with no exposure to the inner workings of this company and without experience or portfolio in management as president and chief executive? It's stupid." Visibly upset, his voice was calm but his body language spoke volumes and his facial expression conveyed exasperation.

Bob Wellington and Darryl started to speak simultaneously. Darryl stopped and deferred to Wellington. "Look, time is getting short, this is already October. We know that Washington is going to make a move soon; he's got to get a candidate elected or face losing his position on the board. Remember, he's retired and without title. Unless he comes up with a new position by December 31st, that's acceptable to the board and Henry, he's out. If he gets a candidate elected as president, he can circumvent that problem."

"You know," Tim said, "if you think about it, it's really kind of curious that he hasn't made his selection known. I mean you'd think he'd want time to introduce whomever he has in mind to the members of the board and do some politicking." Before he could continue, David interrupted.

"Maybe he has a candidate."

"Are you holding out, David? Who is it?" Tim asked.

"No, I don't know anything special, but I agree with you, Tim, Washington has to come up with someone soon." He glanced in Jerry Barton's direction who looked away. "I find it even more curious that

Washington retired from Batem so unexpectedly and at such a young age. Wonder what that's all about?" David couldn't help himself and wanted to give Barton something to stew about.

After agreeing that Corey Topping would have to be considered a candidate in the absence of a better alternative, it was also agreed David and Bob Wellington would have a discussion with Corey about the possibility. In the meantime, they also speculated on who, if anyone, Henry might be thinking about.

Tim and David knew of Henry's meeting with Washington although Henry had not discussed the context of that meeting with them. While Henry, the executive committee, and Mike Spellari were all working behind the scenes there was a definitive change in the feeling on certain floors of the ICA Building. As the days and weeks had gone by more of the company's key people had had contact with Richard Washington. These contacts, however brief, left many with a peculiar feeling of being the enemy in Washington's eyes. He had a way of putting people down or patronizing them that was rude and insensitive. What really hurt was that collectively these people believed in everything ICA and Henry Rothblatt stood for. And Washington poked fun at those beliefs. He ridiculed the believers unmercifully, and pockets of poor morale began to build.

The morale problem was brought to David's attention by an electronic mail message received from Tim. John Morgan, ICA's head claims adjuster and an assistant VP, had met with Tim who detailed their meeting, and it was pretty ugly. Washington had not so subtly suggested that if Morgan could find a way to delay payment on death claims by twenty to thirty days, it could be very advantageous to ICA's bottom line. The proceeds held in an interest bearing account could be a great profit to the company.

According to Tim's EM, Morgan had pointed out to Washington that interest was paid by ICA on all death claims from date of a death and that was true regardless of the date of settlement. He mentioned that it was a fairly common practice of most major life insurance companies. But upon hearing Morgan's reply to his idea, Washington, according to Tim's account, went bananas. He became loud and told Morgan he was an imbecile for agreeing to such a policy. Morgan pointed out that it wasn't his idea or his policy but had been initiated many years earlier. Then Washington continued his tirade outside of Morgan's office. He spoke profanely of ICA and its leaders, from their executive committee to their board. Morgan feared that Washington was literally going to have a stroke. Shaken and appearing confused, Washington told Morgan to pack his bags and get out; naturally, Tim had told him to stay put.

Other reports of Washington's tirades and loss of self-control surfaced and it was getting hairy. Nancy Wagner did not like Richard Washington from her first day of working for him; she saw him as rude, crude, and with a terrible attitude. She was not an indentured servant, she told herself, but that's exactly how she was treated. From the first she had extended herself because of the relationship she thought Henry and Washington had. Day after day of mistreatment, and his abuse of her, had long since convinced her that Washington was not at all what Henry had thought.

In the past couple of weeks Washington had pretty much stopped roaming through the halls of the Home Office. He did not have a high regard for any of the ICA executives, and Jerry Barton, well, he was simply a pawn. Use him as long as he's needed and discard him. This was a naive, ill-equipped group of businessmen, Dick Washington had concluded. They were soft and not at all what he would want as part of his company's culture. He wanted tough-minded, bottom-line people around him. Ruthless was okay too.

Nancy put the mail on his desk; she also made rough drafts of memos and letters that Washington had dictated. Henry dictated and completely trusted Nancy to type, spell-check, and make certain his letters were grammatically correct. Washington wanted to proofread everything.

"Would you like coffee or a cold drink, Mr. Washington?"

"No, no, nothing," he mumbled. When she had left the room he leaned back in the chair behind Henry's desk, closed his eyes, and folded his arms across his forehead. Various thoughts raced through his mind but they quickly began to filter down into only a few.

He was pleased with the way things were progressing. His timetable for the ICA takeover was very much on schedule, and his target date for a board vote was the December meeting. Together with what he and Dena had accomplished thus far, leveraged on top of what they still had to do and would accomplish, they would easily beat the December 31st deadline, thus avoiding any question of his eligibility for the board based on his recent retirement from Batem. He knew that if a vote were held today he could count on eight of thirteen possible votes including his own. President and chairman of the board of one of America's largest life insurance companies sounded good, he thought.

Dena had been of enormous help to him. As head of the University Business School she lent their story enormous credibility. He had once heard it said that every man had a sexual thought about every eight seconds. God, he couldn't get Dena out of his mind, and was certain the eight second theory fit him. He was constantly thinking of the woman. He pictured her in his mind in every conceivable sexual position and situation. He literally could have a self-induced orgasm just thinking about her and all of their past erotic encounters. The heat and eroticism of their relationship evoked in him a desire beyond anything he had ever before experienced.

Eyes shut, in the silence of his office, he allowed his mind to wander to the other woman in his life. That would be Felica, his wife, the princess bitch as he referred to her, though only to himself. More than once he thought about taking ICA public and using the financial windfall to finally get out of a marriage that had been dysfunctional from the start.

Dick and Felica had met through friends. Twenty years ago he was a handsome, early thirties bachelor who had worked his way up the ladder at one of Chicago's major banks. But even then he was impatient, he wanted money and all that riches could give him, and he wanted it all right then, no waiting, no more kissing ass for promotions or raises. To the world he looked like a comer, reasonably prosperous for his station in life, but even then he had the reputation of being a louse when it came to his treatment of women.

On the very first night they had met he and Felicia had made love. She was relatively inexperienced and was somewhat shocked by his violent and intense manner. When she attempted to slow him down and turn what to him was a fuck and nothing more into lovemaking, she was given no quarter, but as the intensity of their experience increased, she found herself getting into his strange exotically intense rhythm.

When Dick discovered that Felicia came from money, his question was, how much? A huge fortune, he was delighted to discover. To his amusement and satisfaction Felicia became addicted to him and his bag of sexual tricks. She had never known anyone so exciting, intense, and assertive. She loved his take charge demeanor, and she adored his lovemaking.

On the other hand, Dick never thought of himself as the marrying kind; bachelorhood was fine with him. He had never really loved a woman; he certainly didn't love Felicia, but her attraction was overwhelming, at least her family's money was.

During the next several months Dick checked out Felicia and her family carefully. He found she had already inherited millions and there was a lot more to come when mommy and daddy passed on. He found her pleasant to look at, but lousy in bed. Great legs, no tits, beaucoup dollars. All in all it was not that bad of a deal. He knew he could have her; all he had to do was ask. Should he? Was her money enough, and would he be able to access it? He had absolutely no desire whatsoever for children and he knew he could never be faithful to her over any extended period of time. After several weeks of consideration, he went for it. With her mommy, daddy, and the whole goddamned family present they were married and had lived sadly ever after.

His parents were not at the wedding; in fact, throughout the courtship, Felicia and her family never met his parents because he had told them they were dead. He had told them a half-truth. His mother died just before they had met. His father, however, was another matter. He was alive, yes, but for all he cared, they were both dead. His father was a drunk who had abused both him and his mother with his mean and obnoxious personality; his mother was a weak and frightened whiner who never came to her own defense, much less his.

As it turned out Felicia was a meal ticket, little more. She wanted no part of any unpleasantness that would upset her world, thus, no divorce. Instead, she allowed him any and all of his dalliances without interference. Shortly after their second year of marriage she uncovered his penchant for extramarital relationships and found herself helpless to do anything about them. She did try for a short while, but his relentless pursuit of women, without any regard for her feelings, had led to their present arrangement. It was agreed between them that he would be discreet and remain available for her whenever she needed an escort to any of her many social, charitable, and political ventures. It worked for him. He would have wanted to attend many of the affairs anyway. They were wonderful occasions to meet those important to his ambitions, as well as to make an occasional social contact of his own.

A sudden increase in the strong Chicago wind blowing hard outside his, or was it Henry's, seventy-ninth floor office suite caused a buzz or howl that stirred Dick Washington from his musings. He wondered, as his senses began to sharpen, if he was really capable of loving anyone. He doubted it. His love, he thought, was for the high that money and power brought him and he was certain that, even though a few matters still needed tending, the ICA deal was going to provide him with both.

CHAPTER 29

The Rothblatts sat at the kitchen table, a colorfully flowered plate of freshly baked chocolate chip cookies and a pot of hot tea in front of them. Ruth had put a small placemat in front of each of them to catch the cookie crumbs and both sipped on straight Lipton Tea, no herbals for either of them. Henry looked stronger and felt better than he had in months. Ruth could sense his buoyancy by the way he had reacted to the last of his treatments.

The doctor told them that the cancer was not exactly in remission, that was probably not possible, but the tumor had been reduced to a manageable size. The question, however, was how quickly it would begin to grow again...and it would grow again. Both Ruth and Henry were cautiously optimistic. There had been cases, such as Henry's, where tumors had taken four or five years to begin their insidious regrowth. In almost every case, once the tumors again began growing they did so rapidly, and it was almost always quickly fatal. But for now Henry felt well and he was finally ready to mount an offensive against Dick Washington. He was fed up with what he had viewed as his defensive behavior, although he had not had much choice, at least not until now. But for Henry Rothblatt it was time to strike back, and he was putting a plan together piece by piece.

"You know, dear," Ruth said, pushing the plate of cookies toward Henry, "it wouldn't hurt a bit if you rested up for a few weeks before getting involved at the office. ICA will still be there for you, with all of its problems intact."

Henry looked about and absently buttoned and unbuttoned the cuff on his cotton flannel, plaid shirt. He waved off the plate of chocolate chip cookies, delicious as they were, and smiled warmly at his wife. "There are two things I need to tell you."

"Have I heard this before?" she asked.

"Maybe once or twice. First, you are very beautiful," he said and squeezed her hand gently, "and second, you worry about me too much." A silence followed, then Henry spoke softly to her as he looked directly into her eyes. Ruth sat still and listened to what she already knew.

"My life, next only to you and the kids, has been the company. The people, Ruth, they are so dear to me. They've been a large and important part of my life. They are in my soul and heart, Ruth." She had heard it before but perhaps he had never been quite this passionate. "I cannot let them all down, and that includes all of our policyholders. They would be hurt and so would our own employees and field people. Ruth, these are people we've vacationed with, had dinner with, laughed with. They know us and we them. I know their kids and they know all about ours."

Henry stood now and walked slowly toward the jalousie windows that were all that stood between him and his beloved ravines. He paused as he scanned the trees now barren of leaves. Then he looked back at Ruth. "This will keep me alive for now. I swear it will, Ruth. I can't rest until order has been brought to this ugly situation. Help me, dear. Please help me. Let me do this at my pace. I don't know how long I've got. Honestly, I don't know. But, I know I'd trade a small amount of time to right this awful situation. I feel so responsible, Ruth. Why didn't I resolve this problem years ago?

"I allowed myself to concentrate only on building the company. My only ambition was to build ICA into a strong and viable company for all of our people. I wanted to provide jobs and security for as many as possible. But why didn't I look to solve the problem of continuation? Why didn't I provide for orderly succession? Why didn't I make certain people were in place behind me, just in case? Now 'just in case' is at hand. I've got to..."

Henry was clearly in despair and as he went on." And then, then, I compound my felony with one of the poorest judgments I've ever made by appointing Washington to his role. My God, what was I thinking of? I should have known better. Ruth, I should have known better."

Ruth walked to him; she saw his sad eyes, his intense face and rigid body and she knew better than to tell him the fault was not his. "You do whatever you feel is necessary," she said. She hugged him and they held each other tightly, closely, lovingly. Then he gently pushed her aside. He excused himself for a few minutes and went to the phone in his den. He dialed, listened, and finally said, "Mike, it's Henry. Can we get together? I want to talk to you and David as soon as possible."

CHAPTER 30

As David's cab headed up Lake Shore Drive toward Wrigleyville it passed the Oak Street Beach. The gray sky filled with puffy, off-white clouds of every shape and size made him realize that as the middle of October approached, winter would be here soon. This winter he knew would be eventful, to say the least. The beach was empt, the waves looked gentle enough, but the water, he was certain, was already ice cold. The outside temperature hovered in the low thirties and that was cold for the city in late afternoon, mid-October.

At Addison Street, the cab broke from Lake Shore Drive's heavy traffic and headed toward David's apartment. He thought the entire city looked unusually gloomy, but was it really the city, or was it he? He felt somewhat depressed, but just thirty minutes later, he sat in his apartment at his cluttered desk with a huge grin on his face. He got up and turned the CD player on. Luther Vandross sang a romantic ballad and David went to the fridge to pull out a beer and plopped into his comfy chair, feet up on the ottoman. He popped open the can, took a long drag, and let out a loud YES! He had just hung up the phone after a twenty minute conversation with Lisa, Lisa Sullivan, to be exact. David Rourke and Lisa Sullivan, it had to be fate. This was the first time he actually had spoken to Lisa in the several weeks since they had first met on his return trip from Scottsdale. She sounded, as she had looked, an angel, an Irish angel he thought. He was not overly religious and had dated girls of every size, shape, and background. Of course they were all lookers, all silky and urban, but Lisa Sullivan, he felt, was someone special. Every instinct told him this was going to be a very special, in fact, a phenomenal experience and relationship. On the phone, she was terrific-sounding, demure and funny with a touch of sexiness. He thought how crazy it was for him to be so enthusiastic about someone he had never really been with, but he couldn't help himself.

They were going to meet Friday night at Centro on Wells Street. He would make reservations for eight o'clock. They would have dinner and get to know each other. He knew that she was dating, but was unattached, and she had not been in a serious relationship in almost two years. She was twenty-seven and originally came from a large family in Woodstock, Vermont. She grew up skiing, which he loved, and she loved everything outdoors, including golf. In short, he thought, they were a perfect fit. His exhilaration was unbounded, and then the phone rang.

"Hi, guy, what's up?" David paused for an answer as Mike Spellari spoke.

"Henry call you for a date when the three of us can get together?"

"Sure did, sounded pretty chipper too."

"Yeah, well, I want to get together with you before then. How's tomorrow? I'll be in the building on business anyway. What's your schedule look like around 10 in the morning?"

"Make it 10:30 and it's a date."

"Done," said Mike. "See you at 10:30, and we'll have our meeting with Henry at lunch time."

"What's the matter, Mike? You sound, I don't know, like hyper, I think."

"Well, let's just say I've got some exciting stuff to share with you, old buddy, and yeah, I'm excited."

"What's up?"

"See you at 10:30, pal," and Mike hung up.

Well, Mike sounded upbeat David thought. Whatever Mike had for him couldn't be too bad, so he settled back, put his feet up and again, and began thinking about Lisa. He tried to visualize her; it had been so long since their meeting. But every time he closed his eyes and attempted to visualize her all he saw was an angel with beautiful red hair and a wonderful smile, no eyes, no nose, and soon he gave up and turned his thoughts to his scheduled visit with Jerry Barton in the morning. It would take place before he met with Mike or Henry. What's with Barton, anyway, he wondered.

CHAPTER 31

In the morning, while David and Jerry Barton were meeting, Henry was in his office for the first time in several weeks. He had called a day or two earlier and asked Nancy to be certain Washington was informed that he was coming. He also told her that he would be in, off and on, for as long as he felt up to it. When Nancy had suggested to Washington that he move to the empty office next door, Dick was the epitome of graciousness. "I'm glad to hear he's feeling up to it." Nancy didn't particularly like the smirk on his face when he said it, and she sensed a feeling of coldness, even ruthlessness, behind the words.

At 8 that morning Henry appeared and Nancy had his coffee, newspaper, mail, and appointment schedule neatly set on his desk. She had been in over the weekend and moved every last vestige of Dick Washington into the office next door. Henry looked about and thanked Nancy as he had her put several appointments on his calendar. That meant they also automatically went on to her computer calendar as well.

"Boris at 9, for twenty minutes, then Bob Wellington at 9:30. I'll be having lunch at noon with David and Mike Spellari. If it's at all possible, Nancy, I'd like to see Mr. Washington around 2 this afternoon for about thirty minutes. I won't accept any meetings after that time. I want to take it easy these first couple of days. I'd also like you to arrange an out of the building executive committee meeting day after tomorrow in the early morning. We'll need one hour. I think that will do it." Then Henry paused, "Nancy, thanks for holding down the fort."

"Henry, may I take a moment or two on an important matter?"

"Of course you can; what is it?"

Nancy sat, hands folded in her lap, and it was clear that she was disturbed. About what, Henry wasn't at all certain; he feared some sort of emotional moment from her. At first she shifted uneasily in her chair in front of his desk, finally reaching down to pick up some papers she had set alongside the chair when she had first been seated. "Henry, I've been with ICA and worked for you for a very long time, and in all that time I've never given you any reason to doubt my trustworthiness."

"Well, that's certainly true."

"I'm afraid now you will have some reason to doubt me."

"Now, Nancy, I doubt that."

He noticed tears were forming in her eyes as she continued. "I've done a terrible thing, but I saw it as an opportunity to help you and ICA, so I did it."

"I'm afraid you've lost me, Nancy. If you think you've helped ICA or me, what have you to be upset about?" He got up from behind his desk and walked around it placing himself on the desktop directly in front of her. He reached down to her lap and took a hand in his. As he gently stroked it, she looked up into his face and felt suddenly calm. He was smiling at her and she noted how handsome he was despite his aging during these past few months. While his eyes were somewhat sunken, they were to her like the eyes of God, her God, holding her hand. "Now tell me, what's this all about?" he said softly not letting her hand go. Slowly she pulled it away from his clasp and handed him a file. He felt her hand slip away and accepted the folder she handed to him.

"What's in here?" he queried.

"Several letters and internal memoranda." Nancy looked quickly down and away from his gaze. "I've stolen them."

"Stolen them? Nancy, how could you steal them? I mean whose are they?"

"They're copies of letters and memos I prepared for Mr. Washington. All of them were marked *Strictly Confidential,* but I thought you should know about them. Henry, I didn't understand everything in them but enough to know that something is going on that you need to know about. I feel you'll want to do something about this, I...just have a feeling." She was now very upset; her eyes brimming with tears while at the same time, strangely, her nervousness seemed to have evaporated and instead was replaced with anger, a great deal of anger. "That man, Richard Washington, is insufferable; he's insensitive and a boor. I don't trust him as far as I can throw him, and on top of it all, his mind is obsessed, there's nothing on it except that woman."

"Woman?"

"Yes, Ms. Callahan."

"Dena Callahan?" As he wiped a tear from her face with tissue from his desk, he looked at her and asked, "Nancy, you're telling me that Dick Washington and Dena Callahan are having an affair?"

"That's exactly what I'm telling you. Oh, Henry, I didn't mean for this to sound so vindictive. Mr. Washington has been rude and crude with me, yes, but I have always felt someone's personal life was their own business. It's just...we... oh, just read the material I've given you. I hope I've done the right thing, and I pray I've misinterpreted what it all means."

With a slight grin, Henry again took Nancy's hand in his. "My dear Nancy, whatever you did was to protect both myself and ICA; I know that. Right or wrong, I know that, and I'll be forever grateful. Let me look over this material and I'll let you know what I make of it. In the meantime, I'm sorry you were mistreated but you're working for me again and very soon things will be as they once were. Now get me that cup of tea. I need to prepare for my lunch with David and Michael."

Nancy started to leave but as she reached the door, she turned, "Incidentally, your appointment with Mr. Washington is at 2 tomorrow afternoon. He said he was unavailable this afternoon. Henry, he had nothing on his calendar."

With a knowing grin, Henry said, "Fine, I'll probably be in about 11 tomorrow, there are some things I need to take care of early. Thank you again, Nancy." She turned and left with a large smile on her face.

At her desk she heaved a sigh of relief and got right to work. At his desk, Henry held the file that he had been given. He glanced at it and slipped it into his briefcase. He sat back behind his desk now and looked at the Chicago skyline, a sensational view of a variety of architectural wonders. He closed his eyes momentarily. He knew he had not told Nancy the truth. He had no matters tomorrow to take care of. He would not come in until 11 so that he could rest and gather himself for what might be a very interesting meeting with Mr. Richard Washington.

CHAPTER 32

Henry's meeting with Nancy had lasted about half an hour; at exactly the same time David had begun his meeting with Jerry Barton.

Just before they were to meet, Barton called David and suggested they change the location of their meeting to the company cafeteria. At 10:30 in the morning there would be almost no one in the eating area. After pouring a cup of coffee for themselves, they found a place at a table in a corner of the room. The window overlooked Rush Street, and David glanced outside and noticed traffic was picking up in anticipation of the approaching holidays.

After a few meaningless pleasantries, David looked intently into Jerry's eyes and said, "Okay, buddy, can you tell me what the hell is going on?"

Jerry, David observed, was as usual dressed to the nines. He was probably the only executive in ICA who gave David a run for the sartorial championship of the Company. He conceded this even though he realized they appreciated clothes that were miles apart in taste and looks.

While David dressed assertively in Canneli and Pal Zilleri, Jerry's clothes were the more form-fitting, European style. Armani and Polo were Barton's taste. David enjoyed stark contrast, black against white or red, navy against yellow, but Jerry went for the monochromatic look. Today he wore a pair of taupe slacks, a dark green, cuff-linked shirt, and a muted nut-colored tie; the shoes were very avant-garde dark tan slip-ons. His jacket had been left in his office.

"There's nothing going on; what do you mean?" asked Barton. He and David had a cordial relationship but they could hardly be called friends. The relationship started and ended at ICA. Over the years there had been only a handful of occasions to see each other outside the office—the wedding of a colleague or some other such event.

"Come on, Jerry, you know exactly what I'm talking about. You're Dick Washington's fair-haired boy." Why he and Jerry had not spent more time together was something David occasionally wondered about. Both were single, both top executives at ICA, and both relatively young and enthusiastic about their work.

Barton spoke in an agitated tone. "First of all, I'm not his fair-haired boy and even if I was, who are you to complain? If you're not Henry's fair-haired boy, you'll do until a better example comes along."

"Yeah, maybe so, but that's Henry, and regardless of who his fair-haired boy is, he's been pretty damn good to both of us. Certainly too good for either of us to give him anything but our total respect and, more importantly, our loyalty."

"Are you saying that I'm disloyal?" Jerry put his coffee cup on the table and leaned toward David. "I think I've been damned loyal. My asking for a little understanding for Dick Washington has as much to do with him being Henry's choice to run things around here in his absence as anything else."

"Maybe," said David, "but I'd like to hear about the anything else."

"What is it you want, David? Sure we've been on opposite sides recently, particularly about Topping, but does that make me disloyal? Not in my book."

David now leaned in a little closer. "Let me cut to the chase. I think you're in bed with Washington. I think he's made some promises to you and I think you've bought them hook, line, and sinker. I asked for this meeting to try to convince you that you're making a mistake. What does he want from you? What's he promised to you? I think I can pretty much guess."

Jerry picked up his coffee cup, took a sip from it, then slowly lowered it and began to speak. "Whatever you think you know is probably bullshit. What the fuck do you know about anything?" He sat straight up in his chair now. His eyes, David saw, had a thin wispy film on them as though in the very first stages of crying. Barton's body tensed as he spoke, and David began to wonder what the hell was going on. It was as though he had touched a raw nerve. For certain the conversation was heating up. "What you know about is the security of Henry's arm around your shoulder. Some of us have to work our asses off to get some recognition, but you just tell him some cute little story, or play a round of golf with him. Well, I'm just looking out for Number One. Make no mistake, David, that's me!

What's wrong with my lobbying for a little attention to my career from someone who's probably going to run this company very soon? Nothing! You'd do the same given half the chance."

"I was given the chance; looks like you've been drafted second."

Barton winced. "What the hell does that mean?"

"It means that when Washington offered me the opportunity to be the puppet president of ICA, I turned him down."

"That's BS," Barton hissed. "Dick told me I was his first choice." Barton's face showed his realization that he may have said too much.

David pressed his advantage. "Yeah, well he lied, surprise! I told him he could go to hell and I stood on Henry's vision of a company and a corporate culture. I told him that the culture of this organization was important to many of us, and he told me that the only culture important to him was profits. We obviously had no meeting of the minds."

Barton looked slightly shaken. "Well, I am surprised about his offer to you, if what you say is true, but I tend to doubt it."

"Oh, it's true! What information have you given him, Jerry? How much of what's been discussed about Corey, for example, does he know?"

"Look, David, I've listened to Dick and his plans, yes. I also admit I told him I'd like to go along for the ride with him, but there were no conditions. I didn't have to give him anything that I didn't want to in return. Mostly, I told him I'd support his positions with the executive committee. I've obviously not done a very good job of that."

Jerry seemed to have calmed down. The realization that he probably was Washington's second choice as a running mate was sobering. Obviously, Washington was just looking for a pipeline of information and anyone would do. Still, he couldn't be certain. Maybe Rourke was lying. "Listen, David, I'm a good soldier and I don't have to apologize for anything. Dick Washington is smart and he knows what he's doing. He'll be good for ICA, good for the company's clients, and good for me. What the hell is wrong with that? It's win-win! But I recognize Henry's been good to me and, in return, I've given him and the company my very best effort, always. But, in my judgment, Henry's finished and I'm not going down with the ship."

"Shut the fuck up!" David surprised himself with his aggressiveness in attacking Jerry and with his tone of voice, but he quickly controlled himself. "Henry is far from finished. Those of us who love this company," David lowered his voice, "are not going to surrender it to some private financier who will break it into little pieces for scrap. Jerry, what's wrong with you? We've been at this for a long time. I know we're not best friends but I also know that we've got plenty of common ground. I can't believe what you're telling me. I'm positive that this company and Henry mean more to you than that. What's really going on?"

"Nothing is going on," Barton shot back. "I'm going to be the next president of ICA. I want that and I'm on track to get it. Dick and I won't be breaking up anything; we'll be building ICA into a great company with aggressive company management. I don't think you and I have anything else to talk about."

With that, Jerry Barton got up, threw his coffee cup into a receptacle, and abruptly left the cafeteria with David sitting dazed and bewildered wondering what the hell had just happened.

CHAPTER 33

At noon, David and Mike met Henry outside his office. With overcoats on they headed toward an elevator for the trip to the garage level where they would pick up Mike's car. They had decided earlier that Manny's would be their luncheon destination. Henry, when asked, had said that he really felt good and wanted a great corned beef sandwich. Ruth would seldom allow that but, though he assured himself he was not giving up, Henry decided he would allow himself this treat while he felt well enough to enjoy it.

Manny's was in the heart of Chicago's Roosevelt Road shopping district. In years past, Roosevelt Road took second place to Maxwell Street, which runs parallel, just a couple of blocks apart. Maxwell Street had been a shopper's paradise offering every kind of soft and hard goods at discount. Predominately Jewish shopkeepers sold their goods at outdoor stands with customers looking for and receiving bargains.

Later, some of the more successful merchants opened indoor stores that spanned the several blocks Maxwell Street ran. Still later, restaurants appeared on nearby Roosevelt Road and the street became famous for its cheesecake and corned beef. In the 1960s, after more than one hundred years of offering a dizzying array of bargains to shoppers, changes began to take place in the name of revitalizing the city. The change didn't come easily, but eventually, after a period when other ethnic groups replaced the mostly Jewish businessmen, and the quality of merchandise fell off drastically, the shops one by one began to close their doors. The smell of food began to dissipate, and in the 1980s Roosevelt Road became the shopping mecca of Chicago's lower west side, and Maxwell Street became history, left with a few hamburger stands and carts selling men's socks at three dollars a dozen.

In the midst of this turmoil, Manny's Restaurant and Cafeteria stood proudly as a fixture in the neighborhood. Located on Jefferson Street, just north of Roosevelt Road, seven days a week, from early morning until early evening, they served food that was famous for both its ethnicity and flavor. Corned beef piled high on rye bread, pastrami, roast beef, thick hand-molded hamburgers with sautéed onions, kishke and potato pancakes, and entrees of portions to provoke bets as to whether the food could or would be finished. Spaghetti and meatballs, chicken, stuffed cabbage, and a variety of soups, kreplack, matzo ball, mushroom barley. It was all rich, tasty, and filling. The restaurant was jammed at noontime with business people who worked in the Loop and the neighborhood's many retail establishments, as well as the customers of those establishments. They stood in long lines with those who just happened to be passing through the neighborhood. Trays in front of them, they walked through the line, smelling the food and wishing they could taste every item. It was this picture that Henry wanted to be a part of today as he, David, and Mike drove down Canal Street looking for a parking place. They would stand in the cafeteria line with the aroma, the excitement, the taste, and the smells that would allow Henry to know that, for now, at least, he was alive.

After finding a table, they set their trays down in front of them. David's and Mike's eyes briefly met and a smile crossed between them. They were looking at a happy Henry Rothblatt. Eyes wide, he was looking at a corned beef sandwich on rye with potato pancakes, "latkes" he called them. The corned beef looked juicy and the latkes perfectly browned and Henry was taking in their taste with his eyes. He sat in his topcoat and Mike helped him shrug out of it, then hung it close by. Henry looked thin but good, yet both Mike and David knew it was probably an illusion or temporary at best.

They talked Cubs, Bulls, Bears, and White Sox. They discussed plans for the coming holidays. As they slowly finished their lunch, Henry's plate still contained half a sandwich; he just couldn't finish it. He sat back, took a sip of his Coke, and then looked intently at the two young men next to him. Just that quickly the entire mood of the lunch changed from three guys enjoying their lunch together, to three men with a serious problem and on a mission to solve it.

"Fellows, I want to thank you both for your help. I'm ready to give this my best effort now. I know it's been difficult for you." Henry took a swig of his Coke, set down his glass, and began telling them of his somewhat mysterious meeting with Nancy Wagner and the mysterious file, earlier that morning.

"What's in the folder?" Both David and Mike asked the question virtually in unison.

"I don't know, I was planning to read it through this evening, at home, but I'll let you know." David marveled at Henry's composure. Had it been he, he could not have waited an instant to tear into the contents of what Nancy had passed onto him. Before he could go any further, David, at Mike's request, told Henry of his less than satisfying visit with Jerry Barton.

"You may be right about Dick offering up Jerry," Henry said. "But if I had to bet, it would be that Dick would select himself as ICA's next president. He won't want to appear presumptuous or greedy to the board, so he'll wave Jerry around. Barton has no chance of securing Dick's nomination; he's just being used."

"I feel kind of sorry for Jerry. I can't quite get a reading on him but something, I'm not certain what, gives me reason to feel badly for him. Maybe it's just that he sees himself as an outsider to all of us." David spoke sincerely.

"Or maybe," Mike spoke up, "you just realize that he's an imbecile to ally himself with that fart Washington."

Henry took back the floor, "Well, the important thing is I've made up my mind as to who we'll be putting in front of the board as our candidate." All the noise in Manny's faded completely into the background. The two younger men stared intently at Henry, their eyes were filled with curiosity. "I'm taking your advice; Corey will be our candidate. His youth and inexperience will be more than compensated for by his intellect and enthusiasm. He's brilliant and personable. He radiates the kind of personal warmth that will give ICA an opportunity to keep its feeling for people alive, but I'm going to have to go into that board room and sell the hell out of him. Washington and Dena Callahan have done a masterful job of selling and whoever their candidate is going to be will stand a very good chance of getting elected. At this point our hands are tied somewhat because we're not even 100 percent certain who their candidate will be; that means we don't know who to campaign against.

"But you seem pretty certain that it is going to be Dick himself,"

Mike observed.

"Doesn't really matter. What we have to make each director understand is that they really won't be voting for a particular individual. They'll be voting for or against taking ICA public."

"That shouldn't be a tough call," said David.

"A lot tougher than you may think." For the first time since the conversation had begun Henry Rothblatt sat tall in his chair and leaned forward. There was a noticeable blaze in his eyes. It was suddenly the old days and Henry had an idea or thought that he felt passionately about. "Dick and Dena have done a good job of lobbying the board. They've planted sugarplums in their heads. Take ICA into demutalization, take it public. You won't be disenfranchising the policyholders; to the contrary, they will each wind up with money in their pockets. Never mind that they won't end up with anything close to what their interest is really worth. Never mind that certain officers and directors will be enriching themselves. What's important is that we will reap windfall profits for ourselves."

Henry's right hand was a claw on top of the table. He unconsciously pushed aside his tray of uneaten food. The blaze in his eyes was now red hot. "We've got to stop them...most of these board members are good people and they're being mislead. It's my fault. I put this bastard in place, now I've got to stop his monstrous plot and I need help."

"You know you can count on us, boss. Mike and I are committed to doing everything we can to help." Mike nodded his agreement as David continued, "Just tell us what to do, what you need."

"What I need you to...what you must do is visit with each board member and tell them our story. Tell them my feelings about demutalization and going public. Tell them it's me talking."

"We'll do that," said Mike. "In the meantime here's some more bedtime reading for you. It's a little gift from a few of your GA's, David and myself." Mike handed Henry the envelope containing the investigator's report on Washington.

"What's this all about"? Henry was eying the envelope.

"Just read it, along with whatever Nancy gave you, tonight." Mike was smiling now. "Could be you're going to have a terrific evening."

David shifted uncomfortably and leaned toward Henry, almost conspiratorialy. "Henry, why did you choose Washington as your interim replacement? You had no idea at all what a snake this guy is? You've known him for some time, haven't you?

"I was wondering when someone would get around to that question; it's not very easy to answer. It's complicated. Yes, I have known Dick for a long time, nearly twenty years. We met when I was first appointed to the presidency of the company. He was our banker. Really, he was our liaison to the bank. Over the next ten years he rose rapidly up the ladder, and about ten years ago he joined Batem Electronics. Until then, we would see each other at occasional business or charity events. Then he joined the country club I belonged to and we would play golf occasionally. Dick is very different from me. The more we saw of each other the more I enjoyed his company. He was articulate, humorous, and I suppose what one might call a rogue. But, he was also intelligent and had excellent business sense. When an opening came up on our board, I selected Dick to fill it. Over the years I would say, particularly at the financial and banking level, he has been a real help to me and ICA."

"And you saw none of the persona he's shown us, during all this time?" David asked.

"Well, I would say that with the passing years and a few personal experiences with him, I've had growing concerns. No, you deserve more of the story, major concerns. For whatever reason, Dick has hardened. The humorous side of him has all but evaporated. I've heard rumors and innuendo but nothing solid. I had made up my mind to dismiss him at the end of this year, then he resigned from Batem and it looked like we would separate from him since he was without appropriate title. That would routinely take place in December, so I just decided to wait it out. The rest you pretty much know. I fell ill and Dick still had the credentials to step in for a period, plus he was not actively employed. He could start right away. Path of least resistance, I suppose. The real problem is less my appointment of him temporarily and more my failure to make certain we would never need to appoint him."

The three men sat for a few minutes; Henry sipped on his Coke, but not a word was spoken.

CHAPTER 34

After a good night's sleep, Henry awoke and hit the shower. Ruth had his breakfast waiting and, for a change, he had a good appetite. Having fallen asleep immediately upon his arrival home, he awoke around 10 P.M. Ruth had made him a bowl of her soup and a plate of homemade chicken salad with a toasted bagel and a glass of milk. While he ate, he read through the file of papers Nancy had so tearfully given to him that afternoon. He also read the private investigator's report Mike had handed to him at their lunch. He knew, of course, that on the next day he had an afternoon meeting with Dick Washington. He had then gone back to sleep and had awakened at about 7 A.M. He would be in his office a lot earlier than he had planned as a result of a certain nervous tension that the best of athletes and actors get just before going on the field or on stage. It was a good kind of tension and Henry looked forward eagerly to his session with Dick. He had planned to try a somewhat friendlier approach than that which he had used at his home several nights earlier when he had gone into the golf tournament.

CHAPTER 35

Mike and David had been quite certain that Henry would read the investigator's report detailing Washington's departure from Batem Electronics and would use it to intimidate him into pulling back. They were more than positive that Henry would be overjoyed when they saw him next. They knew of his meeting with Washington that afternoon and could barely keep from putting an ear to the door. Had they done so, they would have listened to a confident Henry Rothblatt taking on a very cocky and bombastic Dick Washington. They would have heard no mention of an investigator's report, for Henry had decided he could not, would not, use such unseemly information. Henry's confidence, however, was that of a natural leader who felt he could reason and bargain with the best of them.

When Dick arrived several minutes late, Henry took note. He realized it was Washington's way of letting him know that he felt too important to be held to a clock. He also felt Henry's equal, at the very least, Henry thought to himself. The day, this third week of October, was gloomy outside, but Dick had a smile for Henry that said what a great morning it was.

"Good morning," Dick literally sang.

"Good morning, Dick. Sit down, won't you?" Washington took a seat across the room from Henry sitting behind his desk. Smiling, Henry moved to the seating area where the larger man was now seated. Three leather chairs were placed around the coffee table. The chairs were contemporary in 1979 when they first appeared in Henry's office; now they looked a bit dated, but they were in excellent condition and quite comfortable though firm; Henry's back demanded no less.

As Henry seated himself, Nancy appeared and offered coffee or tea. Both men accepted and asked for black regular coffee. When she returned with the two cups and saucers, she set them down, turned, and left the room. Henry spoke first. "Dick, when you and I were at my home last week we didn't accomplish much. I let you know how I felt and you, of course, were indignant. I was hoping that the two of us could have a somewhat more constructive conversation this morning."

"I don't see why not, Henry. What is it you'd like to chat about?"

"Well, to begin with, I'm very interested in your position relative to ICA's place in the market, and then there's your feeling on our succession problem."

"Henry, I won't beat around the bush. I have two basic thoughts on those matters. The first is that after reviewing closely how ICA has been run over the years, I've concluded that it's been grossly mismanaged. My second thought is that any business, where negligence and mismanagement are as apparent as is the case here, must replace those responsible with others who are more able."

"I see, and that means I get replaced for this negligence and mismanagment of the company. Do I understand that correctly?"

"You do understand me perfectly."

"And your proposed solution to this problem is...?" Henry left the question open-ended.

"That ICA replace you and most of your management team with a senior management staff that is experienced and successful at operating a major financial institution such as we have in ICA."

"And exactly what do you see as my transgressions?"

"In the first place, the company's bottom line is atrocious. We could achieve nearly as much simply by investing our present assets in long-term bonds. Describing this company as overstaffed is a kindness, and aggressive fiscal policies are nonexistent. Corrections must be made along with a number of other reforms that would bring ICA into the world of modern business and make us as successful as we should be."

"Who is this *us* you refer to, Dick?"

Washington's mouth gave hint of a faint smile almost as though he were trying to hide it. "Why, ICA, of course," he answered.

"And who is ICA?"

"I don't understand your question, Henry."

"You do, I think, but who is it that makes up the ICA family?"

"Now you see, that's exactly the point, Henry. This isn't a family, dammit, this is a business and should be operated accordingly. The bottom line profits should be the driving concern here, not individuals or groups of people no matter their relationship to the company. Cold, calculated responses to situations must replace this warm fuzzy waffling that is pervasive."

Henry could see he was getting nowhere. With one knee crossed over the other, and leaning back in his chair, he folded his arms contemplatively as though thinking over what had been said. In truth, he was wondering how to respond to Dick, where to take this, so far pointless, conversation next. "And when you are elected president of ICA you'll institute the type of corporate policies you're talking about, I take it."

Dick looked at Henry Rothblatt and decided he would not attempt to play coy. "Absolutely!"

"So, you are proposing yourself for the position."

"Yes."

"And your plan will include a demutualization and taking the company to the market?"

Dick Washington's face now showed some surprise. He picked at imaginary lint on his gray pinstriped suit jacket. "I'm not certain I know what you mean."

"Now, Dick, I think we've been honest with each other so far this morning. You know exactly what I mean. You plan to take this company public and in the process you plan to make certain you enrich yourself handsomely. I hope that presents a clear picture of exactly what I mean."

"Henry, there has been only peripheral thinking on my part of what running this company would mean to me financially. As far as taking ICA public, I won't say the thought hasn't crossed my mind but only that. I've not pursued that concept with any energy."

Henry stood and crossed to his desk. He picked up a file, he sat back on the desktop, opened the file, and began, "You didn't then correspond with James Lewis at Lewis Mancok and Boyne about opening a discussion with them relative to an IPO?"

Before Washinton could respond, Henry continued, "And you have not made inquiries of the law firm of Reed, Mortenson in New York relative to legal matters surrounding your idea?" A now squirming Dick Washington shifted in his chair but said nothing.

Henry crossed back to the sitting area and took his seat, file in hand. "Come on, Dick, let's at least be honest with each other. And on that count, let me continue to be honest with you. I'm very confused and I'm not at all sure why or how we have reached the point we're at. When I took ill, I felt ICA needed an experienced individual, who knew our company, to hold things together until I returned. Truthfully, I saw the role as almost ceremonial in nature. You filled, I thought, the bill very well. You had been a director for several years and had a good handle and feel for who we were, what we did, and what we were trying to accomplish. And Dick, you were a friend, someone I've known for many years. On top of all that you had darn good experience at a corporate level. I knew you had retired and would be available. Obviously, I miscalculated somewhere. Where, Dick? Where did I go wrong? I've thought about that too. Certain facts are evident. You do have strong past experience. You do know ICA, so I have to conclude you just were never the friend I thought of you as being. But why? What have I done that you would take on the role, with the understanding of being an interim president and vice chairman of our board, and then turn around and stab us all in the back this way?"

Dick realized, as Henry finished his question, that Rothblatt had not mentioned taking advantage of his illness. "Stab you in the back? What have I done to any of you? I think you may be looking at your world through rose-colored glasses, Henry. You're the one who should be ashamed. Not only have you allowed, even perpetuated, sub-par earnings for this company; worse yet, you made a CEO's rookie mistake of having absolutely no strategy or plan in place for succession. Had you been hit by a truck and died, this organization might have faced dire consequences. Can you disagree with my assessment?"

Henry didn't have to think it over, he knew Washington was way off in his outlook on the company's earnings. Dick was simply unable to focus on ICA being a life insurance company, not a manufacturer of TV sets. As such, it couldn't prudently invest in instruments of too speculative a nature, looking for large returns. Some insurance companies did do that in the past and paid a dear price. A few might still be doing it today, but most knew that protecting their policyholders and the company's promise to pay was what was important. ICA had to sacrifice return to maintain maximum stability and thus the highest possible financial ratings. The company's expenses were quite low when measured against its peer companies, and its underwriting was conservative, helping it to achieve good mortality results. No, Dick was very wrong, and very uneducated in these matters.

In the few seconds it took Henry to review these facts in his mind, he also realized Washington had scored a bull's eye on his second point, succession planning. He had been so very busy building the infrastructure at ICA, so very busy developing his trilateral marketing and sales concept, that he had failed in providing an important portion of basic business infrastructure, a succession plan.

The trilateral business plan had identified three target markets that ICA would penetrate. Each market would be divided among three separate divisions within the company and each would be relatively independent of the other. If all three divisions had great years, the company operated at maximum financial efficiency. Should one division fare poorly due to that year's economic environment or for other reasons, the company could still do very well. Even if two divisions had poor years, the third division could carry the load because each served a different constituency. It was very unlikely that all three would do poorly simultaneously.

The divisions consisted of what was called within the industry the Ordinary Division, which served upscale clients through an agency or sales system headed by David Rourke, and a Group, or mass marketing, Division headed by Jerry Barton. The division headed by Barton was to sell products and services through financial institutions, such as banks and savings and loans. These institutions had customers who took loans and mortgages from them and would purchase life insurance to cover their debt.

The third division was the Pension Operation and it marketed retirement plans to companies of all sizes throughout the country. When one sector of the economy slowed, such as home building, the group operation might suffer because the financial institutions had fewer mortgages to insure, but the Pension and Ordinary Divisions were there to pick up the slack.

In recent years, the trilateral plan grew another head and ICA began marketing securities on both a wholesale and retail level. The trilateral plan with the addition of the securities business had been a brilliant strategy leading to record sales and profits for twenty successive years; but developing the strategy had a cost.

Henry looked back at his desk and then at Washington. He was thinking of how to answer his question. Did he agree? He wasn't certain. In the few seconds it took to turn back to him, Henry's mind sorted it all out. He had been so wrapped up in taking ICA to its place among its peer companies, so caught up in building the company's infrastructure, and so caught up in planning, that he had virtually ignored putting the people in place to keep everything going after his own retirement or death. Only in the past few years had he begun to think and concern himself over those matters, but it was difficult to play catch-up and now it looked as though time was running out. Did he agree with Dick's assessment he wondered?

"Dick, whether I agree or not is irrelevant. What is relevant is that we must keep this company moving forward and in the right direction."

"And I suppose you, Henry Rothblatt, know what that direction is."

"Yes, I believe I do, and it starts by electing, and supporting Corey Topping as president."

"Who? Who the hell, or should I say, what the hell is a Corey Topping?"

"Corey is a very bright young man who has worked extremely closely with me for over ten years. He's been with ICA as an actuary for nearly twenty years. He understands ICA, who we are, what we are all about, and he has a brilliant ability to think clearly, concisely, and incisively. Corey is also respected by all of us at the executive level as having the potential to be an outstanding leader. He's ..."

Before Henry could get the next sentence out, Dick Washington thumped his hand on the coffee table creating a sound that resonated throughout the room. "Even his name sounds like a squirt of a kid.

For God's sake, Henry, this is a multibillion dollar company, you can't seriously be considering turning it over to a kid. Why, I've never even met this Corey person. I'm on the board, so how important can this character be? Get real, Henry. As far as I'm concerned, this is just additional evidence that times have passed you by. I question your judgment and I don't think you're fit to handle the day-to-day challenges faced by this company."

"But you are?"

Washington grinned slightly and said softly and sarcastically, "I'll tell you all about it at the December board meeting."

"I see," Henry said and leaned back in his chair assuming a relaxed attitude as he realized his plea for unity had gotten nowhere. "There is something we should discuss. I've set December 13th, that's a Monday, for the next board meeting. You may chair the meeting and set the agenda if you like, though the selection of a new president will, of course, be mandatory since I'll be tendering my resignation as president first. You realize, of course, that in the event the board should choose to elect Corey as the company's new president, you will no longer be welcome as a board member of ICA. Of course, without title after December 31st, you wouldn't be allowed to sit in any event."

Henry thought he detected a slight squirming from the thick-bodied man sitting across from him. Washington adjusted his suit pocket handkerchief but made no reply. As Henry stood up he held out his hand and the two men shook, Washington's beefy mitt enveloping Henry's thin bony hand. "I'm sorry, Dick, I'm sorry it's come to this. I was hoping we could have worked this all out. But, mostly I feel saddened at the loss of someone I considered a friend. I trusted you as evidenced by my faith in naming you as vice chairman of the company. I'm distressed, yes, but much more, I'm disappointed."

As their hands unclasped, Dick Washington strode defiantly from Henry's office without a word. December 13th, thought Henry, is not that far away. He silently prayed that David and Mike would have luck in their talks and lobbying efforts with members of the board.

CHAPTER 36

At last it was Friday, and the day seemed interminable to David. He had trouble concentrating on anything but his long awaited date with Lisa. By noon David had given up even trying to work and left the office for home. Once arrived, he undressed and sat in the old comfortable chair he so loved, feet up on the ottoman, no television. Instead he allowed himself to daydream, fantasize, and anticipate the evening ahead. He surprised himself by realizing that his fantasy wasn't sexual. He thought about what Lisa would be wearing, and what they would talk about. Should they discuss families? Of course. Politics? No. Entertainment tastes? Sure.

As he paced about the apartment he wandered into the one area that was always well kept. It could probably get a military medal for neatness. His closet, his pride and joy, contained neatly hung suits, jackets, and slacks, one row of sport shirts, another of shirts to be worn with ties. No, he thought, this was to be dressy casual. He wanted to look neat, laid-back, and like an Adonis. He smiled to himself with that thought, but he did want to connect with Lisa in a very special way.

Later in the afternoon he took a long hot bath; he read a magazine while luxuriating, but couldn't tell you what he had read. He shaved and brushed his hair, slipped on a robe, and relaxed back in his chair. This time he turned on the TV. The five o'clock news came on. "Five o'clock," he exclaimed aloud. It was only five and he had three more hours until he was due at Centro, the restaurant where they would meet for dinner.

Mercifully David dozed off for about an hour. Now, with only two hours to go, he watched Sports Center on ESPN and finally, at long last, it was time to finish dressing. He selected a pair of dark tan trousers with a sleeveless, V-neck, cashmere, chocolate brown sweater. Under the sweater he wore a silk and cotton, collared sports shirt in a light beige tone. The outfit included tan Cole Hahn loafers with tassels, and he slipped on his rust-colored suede sports jacket. He sprayed on cologne then a mint spray for his mouth. He was ready. He decided to cab it over to Wells near Chicago Avenue where the restaurant was located. Arriving fifteen minutes early, he walked around the block twice so he would arrive exactly on time.

The moment he walked through the doors of the restaurant he spotted her— that red hair captivated him. His mouth went dry, even as he plastered a smile on his face. The room, a sort of modern tribute to the Gothic era, faded into the background. The noise, the level was high, suddenly muted. He walked toward her and held out his hand which she took and slightly shook, and as if by magic the noise level went back up and the room brightened.

"Hi," he said.

"Hi, David," she replied.

From that moment he was dizzy with her smile, her voice, and the smell of her. He later recalled that he laughed but damned if he could recall at what. They were seated at a table and each ordered a beer. They drank and looked at each other; they took another sip and looked some more. It was surrealistic, the two of them, just looking at one another. Finally Lisa said, "Well, it's taken forever for us to finally get together."

"From my perspective it's been a long but very worthwhile delay." David spoke and at the same time reached for her hand on the table. "You're really very beautiful, you know. I've thought about you constantly since our meeting on the flight from Phoenix." My God, he thought, he couldn't believe he had admitted that to her. He was concerned that she would think he was some kind of obsessive jerk, or worse.

David need not have worried. Unknown to him Lisa had felt much the same. It was one of those once-in-a-lifetime situations when two young people meet fleetingly yet instantly know they have met their life's true love. Romeo and Juliet, Bonnie and Clyde, and now Lisa and David. Before either of them knew what had happened two hours had passed; they had ordered, eaten, sipped on espresso, and David was now paying the check.

They collected their coats and decided to walk a few blocks in the mid- October's cool night air. They dropped into a small jazz bar David knew. They drank, listened to music, and shared their abbreviated life stories with each other. When David talked about his work, he glowed as he described his relationship with Henry, and she couldn't ever remember a man who seemed so dedicated and loyal to another man. She thought Henry sounded wonderful, part mentor, father, and teacher. She felt happy that David could have such a strong feeling for another man, but she was distressed when David briefly described ICA's present predicament and spoke of Henry's health.

"Henry sounds wonderful, a rare human being these days."

David smiled at her, both in appreciation for her empathy and because he knew in his heart that she would love Henry as much as he did were they to meet. Then, as if by some extrasensory channel they were both linked to, Lisa said, "I'd love to meet him someday."

Without forethought, simply by instinct, David replied, "That's a great idea. Henry would love to meet you. He should get out of the house for an evening if he can. Let me talk to Ruth, that's his wife, maybe we can have dinner with them."

"I'd like that," Lisa smiled. David's heart jumped. He realized they had just made plans for a second date. He leaned back in his chair and stared at her beautiful face, framed by her beautiful, long, straight, red hair with just a hint of a few freckles on her nose; her teeth were the whitest white he had ever seen, making her smile all the more dazzling. He noticed her outfit for the first time all evening. She wore slacks and a jacket under which she had on a turtleneck sweater. It struck him that all evening he had not had one erotic thought toward her. Certainly he had been thinking about her all night, but not sexually, at least not perversely so. How odd that was, he thought. It was exactly then he realized he had fallen in love with her. He desired her but in a wholesome, pure way. That was very different for him. The evening turned out better than anything he could have hoped for, mostly because Lisa had exceeded even his foolish, immature fantasy of her. The evening was also over. As they were ready to leave and get her car, David realized that he had no recollection of what he had eaten, drunk or heard—his every thought had been of her.

Lisa's car came and David tipped the car hiker. He held her hand and said, "Now that we've met and you know I'm not a serial killer,

I hope you'll let me pick you up at your place next time."

"Oh, you're a killer, but I think that will be just fine." Then she turned her dazzling smile on him.

He squeezed her hand and gave her a light kiss on the lips which she accepted. Lisa opened the door to her car, rolled down her window, looked up at David standing there, and said, "I really would love to meet Henry, please call me."

He watched as she slowly drove off and felt like jumping in the air and clicking his heels. Instead he began walking and thinking of Lisa. He did, however, make a mental note to call Ruth and see if he could arrange for the four of them to have dinner.

CHAPTER 37

The first week of November arrived. David's days had been filled with lunches and dinners with ICA board members. Mike Spellari and David were doing their best to bring Henry's story to the board. They also used the opportunity to introduce Corey Topping. David felt as though they had all made a good impression though he wasn't the least bit sure where many of the directors stood. David found them difficult to read. Mike was more cynical and negative in his assessment of their mission.

David's role was to reduce the relationship tension with a good story and to keep the meeting flowing. Mike impressed on each member the importance of retaining the company's mutuality and culture. Corey tried to be personable and make the best possible impression. He was not certain how far to push his business skills and background on these men. He felt strongly that Henry's endorsement of him was just short of being enough, but Corey couldn't and didn't know how skilled Dick Washington and Dena Callahan could be. The degree of their success in manipulating the board was amazing, to say the least. They did their homework and appealed to each director's personal taste. They were masterful and convincing. All this was beyond anything the three young men could have believed.

David found time to convince Ruth that she and Henry should have an evening out. To his surprise, Ruth agreed and said she felt it would do Henry a world of good, and a date was set for the coming Friday evening. It was already Wednesday and David didn't know which he looked forward to more, being with Henry and Ruth or seeing Lisa again. He decided the whole thing was wonderful and as he sat in his chair in front of the TV, Heinie in hand, he was glad Henry and Lisa would meet. Lisa would love Henry, he knew, and Henry would be knocked out by her. He drifted into a light sleep and didn't hear the Tonight Show or later Conan O'Brien but at 1:30 A.M. the shrill ring of his telephone gave him an abrupt start.

At first disoriented David quickly regained his composure and sat up. He reached for the portable phone and pressed the on button.

"Hello," he said in a voice that betrayed that he had been awakened from his sleep.

"David?"

"Yeah, who's this?"

"Boris."

"Boris? Boris who?"

"Come on David, wake up, Boris Howe."

"Boris, it's nearly 2 in the morning," David observed as he glanced at his wrist watch. "What's going on, is there a problem, are you okay?"

"I'm fine David, but yes, there is a problem." A short pause then, "David, can you meet me at the Mirage Bar over on Halsted and Lincoln"?

"Now?" asked David.

"Right now, as soon as you can!   Don't ask any questions, just get over here, okay?"

"Boris, what the hell is this all..."

David was cut off. "Just get here now. Now, David! Quickly!"

It took David less than ten minutes to throw on a pair of jeans and a sweat shirt. After slipping on a pair of gym shoes, he bounded down the stairs of his apartment and headed for his car. It was only another ten minutes at that time of the morning to reach the bar Boris had called from. He found a place to park on the street just a few paces from the front entrance of the Mirage. Although David had never been inside, he surmised from what anecdotal evidence he observed, that it was a gay bar. The neighborhood, and Boris' gay lifestyle, were his clues though a few men standing just outside the bar gave reinforced his conclusion.

Inside it was dark with dim purplish lighting. A stereo played Sinatra from one of his romance albums. Under other circumstances David could have listened, been entertained, but he concentrated on looking for Boris. His eyes found him at the bar sipping a drink and as Boris looked up and saw him, David looked past him and was stunned. On a stool next to Boris was a familiar figure, sitting with his tie pulled down and collar open and his eyes red-rimmed. It was a drunken Jerry Barton.

"Jerry!" David said in astonishment, his surprise dissipated when almost instantly the puzzle began to fall into place. No wonder he had never run into Jerry socially. While he hadn't ever been able to put his finger on it, now the scenario seemed crystal clear. Why hadn't he picked up on the all too abundant clues, he wondered. With equal speed, his mind tried to calculate the problem. Why the call from Boris and what was with Barton?

Jerry seemed in a highly emotional state. His head hung and he mumbled incoherently while he cried uncontrollably, suddenly stopping to just stare into space.

Boris put his arm out to stop David as he moved toward Barton. "Let's talk, David," he gently said and pulled the young man's arm so that David now stood next to Boris. "Good Lord, what happened to him?" David gestured toward Barton.

"It's a long story, but the bottom line is he was hit by a runaway train, the Dick Washington Special."

"What's Washington got to do with this?"

Boris looked at David with a steady gaze. "I wouldn't have dragged you out of bed at this time of morning just because Barton hung one on. He called me here about 11 and sounded pretty shaken."

David wanted to ask how Jerry knew Boris would be at the Mirage but before the question could form on his lips, his mind knew the answer so he remained silent. Boris continued, "I told him I'd wait for him and when he arrived he was pretty much in the condition you see him in now. He's only had a couple of drinks since he got here. It seems Jerry saw Washington earlier in the evening and told him he wanted out from their deal. He says he didn't want to be a pipeline of information for him, and he told him he knew that he had offered the presidency of ICA to you before he'd come to him. Apparently Washington laughed at him and told him it didn't matter any more. Dick said he would be the next president of ICA and there wouldn't be room for a fag like Barton."

"Boris," David asked, "you knew that Jerry was gay?"

"Yeah, for a few years. He's been buried in the closet though."

"Well, how did Washington know?"

Slowly, Jerry Barton had gotten up from his stool and moved nearer to the two men. He was listening intently. Now he spoke, his voice weak and sorrowful, "He fucking knows everything. He's had everyone investigated who he thought could be a problem or who he wanted to get something on." The two men turned their eyes toward Jerry, who looked disheveled and tired, but as he spoke, his voice had become stronger. He looked directly at David. "You were right, you know. I was his spy. I told him about every conversation the executive committee ever had; I fed them everything."

"But why?" David asked.

Before Jerry could answer Boris said, "Blackmail."

"Blackmail?" David looked slightly puzzled, almost as though he knew the answer to his question but couldn't quite bring himself to believe it, and didn't want to.

"Jerry's choice was to remain quiet about his sexual preference," said Boris. "Washington found out about him and threatened to use the information if Jerry didn't cooperate, simple as that."

Jerry spoke again, this time with tears streaming down his face but in a clear strong voice. "I went to his place tonight. He invited me in and I began to tell him how I felt. I had downed a few scotches and was feeling no pain. I told him I didn't care if he did tell people about me, I just couldn't go on betraying all of you, Henry, ICA. I hated myself. As I was talking with him, Dena Callahan walked in from another room. She had on a robe, and she didn't say anything at first, she just sat in a chair. Actually the conversation with Washington wasn't going too badly. He wasn't happy, but he seemed kind of unbothered by it all. After I told him how I felt and he told me where I could get off, I even thought he might forget any notion of outing me."

David glanced at Boris who held up a finger to his lips and gestured with his head toward Barton as if to say to David, listen, there's more. Jerry was going on but as though he were in a trance. In his mind he was replaying the scene at Washington's home.

"So, Jerry, you don't want to be part of our team? You don't want to play ball with us?" Dena was speaking. "Well, maybe there are some other games you'd like to play?"

"I don't think Jerry has ever played some of the games we like, darling. Am I mistaken, Jerry?" Dick moved into Jerry's space and face.

Dena, robe now fully framing her slender, soft body stepped close to the two men and Jerry noticed the heat that her body generated. "Jerry, although we may not any longer have a business relationship, I do hope we can be friends, good, close friends."

"I'm leaving," Jerry remembered muttering, but before he could take a step, Dena sneaked her arms around his neck and pressed close to him. "Come on Jerry, have you ever experienced a woman? You might find it quite nice, you know. Many of my friends go both ways. Have you ever felt a woman's breasts, Jerry?" She placed his hand on her right breast.

Dick Washington had stepped back to take in the picture and hissed, "Go ahead, Jerry, don't be afraid."

"Have you ever felt yourself slide deep inside a woman?" Dena asked. There was no smile on her face; instead she looked deadly serious. She really wanted him. This was a new challenge and a new conquest, she thought. Jerry saw it in her face and he panicked.

"Let me go. Get out of my way." As he started to turn away, Washington pushed him back to the place where he had been.

"Get out of my way, Dick."

Once again Barton began to turn and leave; this time Dick Washington pushed the smaller man down on the floor and began to pull on Jerry's belt as the man lay on his back. Jerry was confused and dazed, unbelieving of what he saw coming. Washington wanted this; he wanted Dena to have sex with him. This would be rape, he remembered thinking. He struggled as Washington began pulling down Jerry's slacks; in the meantime Dena's robe was thrown aside as she stood over Jerry. Tears began to form in the younger man's eyes as Dick finished pulling Jerry's pants from his legs. Dena stepped back, leaned over, and yanked the young man's boots off his feet. As she did this, a taunting smile appeared on her face. Washington laughed when he saw tears. Jerry's emotional state seemed to give both Dena and Dick a kick. They gave no quarter, much less show any remorse. To both of them this was a blast; it was fun. They understood full well that to Jerry Barton this was an emotionally devastating experience. They watched him squirm under Washington's strong hold while Dena teased his body. He cried out in pain which, though emotional, felt physical, and his entire body was bathed in sweat.

Jerry let out a muted cry and slowly began to come back to the present. He looked around and realized that Boris and David were at his side, and he was suddenly sober. He was ashamed and angry. David walked to him and, though Jerry tried to shrug him off, David put his arm around his shoulder. "Jerry, the two of them are sick fucks; don't let them destroy you." He turned to Boris, "Take him home, make certain he's okay."

"Where are you going, David?"

"I'm got some medicine to deliver to a couple of sick morons."

"David, don't do that. We've worked hard to keep this out of the spotlight; the cops come, there's an arrest, everything is out in the open. Don't do it, David."

"I'll talk with you in the morning Boris, take care of him."

CHAPTER 38

David had fumed for days after his early morning visit to the Mirage. Though he had seriously considered a visit to Dick Washington's home that same night, he realized discretion was probably the better part of valor. He had wanted to punch Washington's lights out or, at the very least, let him know what a perverted shit he was. He wanted to taunt him telling him that he and others knew about his so-called retirement from Batem. But in the end, David convinced himself it was better to keep that to himself, especially since Henry was steadfast in his refusal to use the information. Furthermore, for Jerry Barton's sake, it would be better if Henry and others weren't aware of what had occurred, or of Jerry's sexual preference. It was, after all, Barton's own business.

David hadn't seen Jerry for a few days but they did talk on the phone. Jerry called and thanked David; he also asked for his silence and discretion. David assured him that he wouldn't discuss the matter with anyone. His decision not to find Washington and beat him to a pulp was, he now felt, good judgment on his part.

The board meeting was only a week away, and as he walked down Michigan Avenue toward a lunch with Bob Wellington and Boris Howe at the Ritz Carlton Café, the cold November air cleared David's head momentarily. He thought about Friday night coming up when Lisa and he would have dinner at the Capitol Grille with Ruth and Henry. All four people, he knew, were looking forward to the event. Henry wanted a great steak and looked forward to meeting Lisa, and Ruth looked forward to a night out, rare in her life these past months. Lisa wanted to meet the man David so obviously admired, and David wanted to be with Lisa again and have her share his affection for Ruth and Henry.

Crossing Michigan at Chicago Avenue, David walked the last block to the Water Tower and across to the Ritz. As he was finishing the walk, he recalled his recent phone conversations with Lisa. She had left for a three-day West coast trip, but they spoke each night, more than once on a couple of evenings. On both of those nights he had called her, finished their conversation, and then she called him back a couple of hours later. Their conversations were fun and warm. In every single conversation Lisa asked more and more questions about Henry and his relationship with David. David took her interest as more evidence of her loving nature and he cared more for her by the minute.

At lunch, with Bob and Boris, they discussed the protocols and agenda for the coming board meeting, a week from Monday. Now, just a few days away, David and Mike agreed they had not made overwhelming progress toward convincing the board that Corey Topping was a viable candidate in opposition to Dick Washington. They had a few votes, they knew, and a few more were undecided, but the majority of the board were blinded by what they perceived as Washington's savvy and knowledge of ICA. His picture of a great windfall to the board's directors, if they took the company public, didn't hurt his case.

David, especially, wanted this lunch to thank Boris for a couple of things: first, his interest and discretion where Jerry Barton was concerned, but of equal importance David's realization that, with all that had transpired, not a word had leaked to the press. That kind of damage control, he knew, was due only to Boris' skills as ICA's vice president of public and media relations.

During lunch, Bob Wellington told them that, although Henry had given Washington the authority to set the agenda for the board meeting, Dick had turned that task over to Bob with the admonition to be damn certain to include the vote for president. Bob mentioned Henry would nominate Corey as a candidate, and the second would come from Wellington himself. Dick Washington would arrange for his own nomination. There would be some perfunctory time spent before the call for the vote on such items as the reading of the minutes and new and old business. He didn't expect much else to come up; the vote was definitely the issue at this meeting.

All of the board members had been sent notices of the meeting, and in an unusual reaction, every director had responded affirmatively. It seemed no one wanted to miss this particular session. Usually someone was out of town or had urgent business, but not this time. As they had lunch, they discussed their chances to save ICA and were not overly optimistic.

David detailed some of the meetings he, Mike, and Corey had with several directors. He explained that all were most cordial, but there was an undercurrent with several that was difficult to explain or describe. Only after most of the meetings had taken place did the three men realize that the common denominator of resistance was not to Corey, but, in some cases, was an unconscious embracing of the windfall Dick and Dena had unfolded to each member. Stock that would be worth hundreds of thousands of dollars, in some cases worth millions, was what was providing their biggest obstacle. Each man, however, held out the hope for a miracle.

Most of the board were good, sincere, and honest people. Many had served as ICA directors for several years or longer. While they may not have completely understood the inner workings at the company, most had a good fundamental knowledge of how the company worked and all were highly successful running a variety of businesses, from banking to technology, and most everything in between.

It was the entrepreneurship that only a few on the board really were able to deal with. These were people who ran companies where everyone was an employee. The sales force of "the Field" as it was commonly referred to was a different ballgame for them. The Field, the men and women who made it happen, were by contract independent contractors and that meant they essentially ran their own shows.

Those on the board, who truly understood that, could only admire the manner in which Henry had, over a period of years, convinced these individuals that they were in a very real sense partners in ICA. Henry Rothblatt was both their partner and leader. What was good for the policyholders was good for ICA, and therefore was good for the Field. In all the years of Henry's stewardship, he never failed to listen to the Field and consider their position, and they admired him for it.

While members of the board admired not only Henry's leadership skills but his business acumen and visionary abilities as well, Washington and Dena had, nonetheless, been extremely convincing that his sickness, along with the drugs he was on, may have in some way impaired his judgment, for the time being, at least. David and Mike could not be sure of how certain directors were thinking and had so advised Henry.

Would Henry be strong enough to attend the board meeting, Boris had wondered? "If he has to be carried in on a stretcher, he'll be there," David had replied.

After more conversation about what the future might hold for all of them and ICA, the three men headed back to the office. David lingered momentarily as he remembered that in just two days he and Lisa would be having dinner with Henry and Ruth and that thought made him smile. He knew she would charm them as she had him. He realized that his suddenly buoyant spirit was caused less by the thought of dinner and more by the thought of once again being with his Irish princess. He was grinning as he headed back to the ICA building.

CHAPTER 39

Henry and Ruth arrived a few minutes early. The distinguished-looking couple were shown to the table David had reserved in his name at the Capitol Grille. Ruth gave the waiter her drink order, a Merlot, while Henry asked for his usual Diet Coke. While the Rothblatts held hands and made small talk, David was pulling up outside the trendy windy city restaurant. Lisa, as it turned out, was only ten minutes from David's apartment and, to his delight, was absolutely punctual, waiting outside her building at exactly the agreed upon time. He couldn't help wondering if he would see her apartment later that evening. On the way to the restaurant, the sharp-looking young man had smiled to himself as he imagined the meeting about to take place. Every instinct told him this was going to be a great evening. Lisa and David made their own small talk on the short ride and were now pulling up to the doorman standing outside the Grille.

After checking the car, then their coats, they walked toward the table where Lisa took note of a wonderful looking man and woman, who turned out to be Ruth and Henry Rothblatt. Her every instinct had told her this was Henry Rothblatt and she was correct. She was stunned at how accurately David had described Henry, who stood and took her hand. "This is a special treat for me, Lisa. David has told me so much about you that I feel as though you're an old friend."

"Thank you, Henry, I could say exactly the same about you." After Lisa exchanged hellos and shook Ruth's hand, and after David kissed Ruth on the cheek, the younger couple took their seats. In a few seconds a waiter appeared to take their drink orders. Glancing at Ruth's Merlot, Lisa followed suit. "I'm a little disappointed, Lisa," Henry offered, "David told me you were a two-fisted beer-drinker."

Looking up at the waiter Lisa said, "I'll change mine to a Miller Lite." They all laughed. After David ordered a Heineken, Henry asked for another Diet Coke. Even when he had been perfectly well, he seldom drank hard liquor, an occasional scotch or brandy, and never alone. Finally, the four of them sat back and let the picture sink in. Each noted the beauty of their surroundings, rich woods and

135

leathers, plenty of room for each table or booth.

The ambiance combined with smartly attentive servers and the Grille's reputation for its food promised to make this the great night David had anticipated. This was especially so, David thought, because already Henry and Lisa seemed to be hitting it off.

"I love your sweater, dear," Ruth had mentioned to Lisa.

"I bought it on one of my trips to Hong Kong."

"That's right. David mentioned you were a flight attendant, but you look too young to have the seniority I understand it takes to pick up overseas flights," commented Henry.

"I started when I was only fifteen," Lisa joked. She looked across the table at the older man while allowing David to hold her hand on top of the table. She saw a man who she could tell was once quite handsome though he now looked frail and had a thinning hairline. He had a craggy almost outdoorsman look to him, and Lisa was well aware of a pervasive charm and warmth he somehow exuded, even while saying little. Her heart was sad as she realized she was looking at a man who was living out his last days.

Henry was animated, for Henry, thought David. He and Ruth liked Lisa, he was certain, and, as he observed Lisa, he knew instantly she was as in love with Henry as he was. He tried hard to listen to the ebb and flow of conversation, but found it difficult; his attention was constantly drawn to his date's beautiful face. At last a waiter approached and, after mentioning a few specials, he took each of their orders. All of them ordered steak. Henry, as usual, ordered his well done. The waiter flinched but kept smiling. Lisa caught his look and laughed lightly when she added, "Make mine well done, too."

As the waiter left their table, Henry leaned across, looked into her eyes and said, "Young lady, if you think he's upset with the way I ordered my steak, wait until I ask him for ketchup."

Lisa laughed again, and this time she put an elbow into David's ribs; the gesture somehow caught David's funny bone and he became hysterical. As is often the case, the laughter became contagious and the whole table was rocking. Those at the next table looked over and saw four people having a genuinely good time.

After they had finished their meals and were each sipping coffee, the mood at the table, which had been quite festive turned quiet, as if each of them was caught up in his or her own thoughts.

Lisa broke the silence with a question. "Henry, I hope I'm not being too rude or presumptuous when I ask this question but, well, I guess you could say I'm curious, interested actually. Are you going to be able to save ICA? David's given me an overview of what's happening, it all seems so horrible."

Lisa watched as Henry glanced first at Ruth and then at David. At last Henry's gaze fell on Lisa. His thin smile was betrayed by his sad eyes. "I think we'll do just fine." Henry spoke without any hint of conviction. "David and his associates have worked hard on getting our story told; I'm certain we'll be successful."

All in all, that was pretty unconvincing, David thought. "We've done out best, Henry, we really have, but it's kind of like having an enlisted man handing out the war plan. Everything he says is right, but somehow the troops aren't necessarily convinced; they're waiting to hear from the general." David looked directly at Henry, looking for some sign of fight in his friend.

"Well, we're all doing the best we can," said Henry as he took a sip of his coffee. Setting down his cup, he heard the young woman across from him say, "With all you've done over the years for so many people, David has told me so many stories, I would think it would all count for something. From the way David has explained it to me, you're a very unusual leader, someone who commands the utmost loyalty and who has given loyalty in return. That must count for something."

Ruth Rothblatt took their conversation in and said nothing. She just wanted to keep her husband as long as possible but she became noticeably more attentive as Lisa had gone on. David extolled Henry's virtues and told story after story of how, though Henry didn't let his heart rule his decisions, he always listened to what his heart had to say and weighed it on balance with whatever his brain was telling him. The stories were nearly endless and thirty minutes later David was winding up yet another story of Henry's thoughtfulness and generosity when Henry interrupted saying, "I've got to get to bed, I haven't been out this late in a long time." Henry seemed genuinely pleased with his evening out, but was truly exhausted; he was also tired of being canonized.

As they gathered their coats and headed toward the front door to retrieve their cars, Ruth slid next to David and quietly asked if he would be in his office on Monday. David acknowledged he would be, and Ruth walked quickly away to join her husband. Strange, David thought momentarily, but then dismissed the incident.

Once in the car he looked at Lisa and said, "Well?"

"Oh, David, he's wonderful. He's everything that you said he was. He's really dear; I'm so upset for him. I think I could almost handle his illness and death but the thought of losing his company, it just isn't fair. Oh my, I'm sorry." She was crying now, full blown. She was genuinely sad and David was moved. As he pulled away from the restaurant he slid his arm around her shoulders and pulled her to him. She laid her head on his shoulder still weeping silently. David squeezed her shoulder gently and headed toward her apartment. As they drove along he knew tonight would not be their first time together. It just didn't seem appropriate somehow. He also knew he was very much in love. Tears had formed in his own eyes. Why, he wondered? Because of her? Because of Henry? He realized it was because of them both. He loved each of them; he loved them both.

CHAPTER 40

At exactly 10:30 on Monday morning Ruth Rothblatt called David at his office. "David, I want to see you." They made a date to meet later in the afternoon. Henry would have left for home.

After his meeting with Ruth, David sat behind his desk leaning back in his black, leather, executive chair. He pulled a paperclip open, absently. "Damn," he muttered to no one. "Damn, Henry's one smart dude, but she's not too shabby."

David stood and walked to a window, and looking out at nothing in particular, he suddenly broke into a smile as he though about Ruth's visit. "Damn, Ruth, damn."

Ruth had started their meeting by reminiscing about all the wonderful times she and Henry had attending meetings and conventions. She told David, who already knew, how those times were among Henry's happiest. They remembered and laughed over the time the company had made arrangements for a trip on an old boat between St. Thomas and San Juan, Puerto Rico. Everyone had flown over to do some shopping in the morning, spend the day in St. Thomas, and board the boat for cocktails and the ride back to San Juan. The sea was a bit choppy and the late afternoon and early evening grew chilly on deck where most everyone congregated. Suddenly, above the wind a woman's voice shouted, "Oh, my God, she's having her baby!"

A wife of one of the younger agents at the convention was pregnant, but not for long. The long day and rough sea were enough to put her into labor, and the baby came. Ruth and Henry were doctor and nurse, cool and in control. The beautiful little boy was delivered without incident, wrapped in jackets and coats, and an hour later taken to a hospital in San Juan.

The next morning at the convention meeting, the father of the baby asked for a moment of the audience's time and promptly announced mother and baby were doing great, and that, by the way, mom and dad had named the baby Henry. It was a magical moment. There was wild applause and at least half of the women cried hysterically.

"Damn, Ruth, damn."

Ruth had made special note of the fact that Henry enjoyed himself at these meetings because he felt a real admiration for those independent entrepreneurs that made up the field force, especially his general agents. He admired their courage in starting and building field offices and their willingness to take risks.

At first David thought it a strange thing for Ruth to bring up. But then, Ruth mentioned—she made it seem in passing—that Henry also appreciated his G.A's importance to the company. After all, she remarked, "They were the link and contact between ICA and the policyholder. Isn't that true, David? Imagine what could happen if they weren't around."

David didn't catch on at first, but when she continued with, "They loved each other so much, the Field and Henry, they would do anything for each other," the whole idea exploded in David's head. Now standing at his office window he couldn't wait to get hold of Mike.

PART III
DECEMBER 1996

CHAPTER 41

On Monday, December 5th, the first Monday of December, the day was unusually bleak. A gray mist hung over the city and the early morning air was chilled. As Nancy Wagner arrived at the ICA building, she was happy to step inside, out of the cold and damp. Snow was predicted for the afternoon and she was prepared with her boots which she carried in a small Marshall Fields shopping bag. A shopping trip at Fields would have been a far better alternative than the day she was about to face.

Bob Wellington rode the elevator down to the sixth floor for a chat with Boris. His face showed his anxiety about what lay ahead. Nonetheless, he was prepared to assume his role. He and Boris would discuss the possible dissemination of various pieces of information that could come out of the afternoon's board meeting. Boris also had printed agendas that would be on the table in front of each director's chair as the meeting participants arrived.

The protocol was that any director could ask for an item to be included on the agenda as long as the secretary and chairman were notified at least three days in advance of the meeting.

David was in his office at 8 A.M. and was just reaching for his phone when he spotted Tim Walker walking by his door. He called out, "Tim!" With a coffee cup in his hand Tim backed up a few steps and stood in David's doorway.

"Big day, you guys ready?"

"As much as we can be. Tim, I just wanted you to know that a few of us will be here while the board meets. We kind of figured we'd share the tension."

Tim nodded his understanding and gave the thumbs up sign.

"I'll be here," he said, as he moved on.

As David reached for the phone, Jerry Barton poked his head in the door. "Mind if I come up here about 3:30? I don't think I can wait by myself, too nervous."

"Absolutely, Jerry, how are you doing? You okay?"

"I'm fine David; thanks for asking. I'll see you this afternoon."

For the third time David reached for the phone. This time he dialed a four-digit number, which meant it was an internal call. He got Corey Topping's voice mail. "Call me, it's David. I'm a nervous wreck," was the only message he left.

Outside, the day required overcoats, gloves, and scarves. Only such items would protect someone from the bitter wind that blew on Michigan Avenue. Henry's car pulled into the building's garage at about the same time Richard Washington slid his into a stall. Henry alighted and headed toward the bank of elevators. He carried no briefcase, only the gloves in his hand.

Washington pressed the lock button on his remote and the doors of his Mercedes snapped into the locked position. He walked away from the auto with a large, flat briefcase and headed for the exact spot where Henry now stood, patiently waiting to be taken to the seventy-ninth floor. As Dick entered the vestibule that contained the elevator bank, the two men stood facing each other and said nothing for a moment, each collecting his thoughts.

"Good morning, Dick," Henry said with no rancor or sentiment in his voice. It was a straightforward remark.

"Hello, Henry," was Washington's terse reply. Then as they rode up he said, "Big day."

Henry's only reply was to turn his head ever so slightly toward the other man and nod his head imperceptibly to acknowledge the remark. Then his eyes looked straight forward at the walnut-paneled, brass-trimmed elevator doors.

By now December had become what most Decembers are like in Chicago, very cold with a number of snow flurries, though nothing had stuck to the ground thus far. Henry's suburban home on the ravines of Highland Park offered him warmth at the fireplace and warmth from Ruth. Both of them knew he was slipping a little each day. Henry Rothblatt was a man exhausted by the medications, chemotherapy, and radiation he had undergone. His body wore the scars of intravenous treatments and his clothes hung loosely as his weight continued to drop. Just two days ago, Dr. Weinstein had told him he had three months at most, probably a little less. But he was also a highly motivated man as the elevator cabin slowed and the door folded back at the seventy-ninth floor. The two warriors stepped out and each headed to their respective offices without another word passing between them.

Warriors they were, indeed. For Washington it was survival, and the instinct for survival was mighty. If he could pull this off and get himself elected as ICA's new president, his worries would be over. He knew, of course, that in the improbable event the board did not elect him as ICA's new leader, replacing Henry, then his days at ICA would be over and he would be finished. Should ICA announce that Washington was being forced from their board, as a result of having been unable to secure a position comparable to his role at Batem, then many of those other boards of which he was a member would, in all likelihood, also remove him as one of their directors as well. This was do or die, notwithstanding the personal fortune to be made if he were able to take ICA public. This would be an initial public offering to end all IPO's and he would wind up with the titles of President and CEO, then eventually, Chairman of the Board. He'd also end up with Dena. He could not forget Dena; he was consumed with her. His days and nights were a stream of erotic thoughts of her. But, today, he was a warrior and he was going to war. The battle would begin at exactly 4 this afternoon.

Washington's opponent was, of course, Henry Rothblatt who himself was ready for battle. He had slept little the last few nights, tossing and turning, thinking and planning. The restlessness was a result of his struggle to keep his mind clear. The doctors had given him pain medication but it made him groggy and his mind fuzzy. Fortunately, there was not as yet much pain, and he needed the drugs only intermittently. He had, however, taken himself off all the pain medication three days ago so that he would be able to concentrate with a mind that was clear and active when the first shot was fired this afternoon.

Henry lacked sound sleep. It had to do with the constant memories and thoughts of Ruth, his children and grandchildren. His heart broke, not for himself, but for the unbearable sadness he knew Ruth would shortly face. She would be well cared for and want for little, but she would miss him enormously, he knew. Ruth understood him and he knew her, they were like one person in two bodies. The kids would have a slightly easier time though they would dread not having him around to counsel and to kibbitz with. They sometimes took advantage of him, but he loved it, and they put back love, affection, and caring in measure greater even than what they took. He would close his eyes and see them all on their trip to Israel, which he and Ruth had spent months planning. He could smell them all; he could smell Ruth's cooking. Still, he was haunted by what a few people were trying to do with his company, steal it, change it, destroy it. They wanted to rob ICA of its culture, of its caring for its people and its policyholders. His mission today was also to win a war, and he had always been the ultimate warrior. The question was did he have the strength, much less the ammunition, to win this war? The strength he knew he could muster and will to himself, the ammunition might be another story.

CHAPTER 42

At about te10 A.M., Mike Spellari received a Federal Express package at his office. His secretary brought it to him and he opened it and withdrew a letter. He unfolded it, glanced at it, refolded it, and slipped it into an envelope. He put the envelope into his inside suit pocket, then he picked up the phone and placed a call. In a few seconds David answered and Mike said, "I've got it." Mike listened for a moment and then said, "I'll see you at one." He replaced the receiver, sat back in his chair, and thought deeply for a few minutes. He took the envelope out of his pocket, took out the letter, unfolded it, and, pen in hand, wrote on it. Then he refolded it, put it back in its envelope, and replaced it in his pocket. There was some business to take care of before he met David at one o'clock. As he stepped into his private washroom to make certain he was put together, he looked in the mirror and noticed a smile on his face. "Damn," he said to no one, "you are one good-looking dude."

David had placed the conference call to his seven leading general agents around the country. They were located in Detroit, Los Angeles, Cleveland, Minneapolis, San Francisco, Atlanta, and, of course, Mike in Chicago. All had taken his call at the same time with only an hour's notice. They came out of client meetings and training sessions, and off the golf course.

Mike did the talking. They were told Henry was in trouble. ICA needed them, and he spelled out a bold plan to save the company. There was risk, huge risk to each of them, and to a man, without hesitation, the group agreed to take the risk. They would have done almost anything for Henry Rothblatt.

CHAPTER 43

At 10:45, Mike, David, and Bob Wellington sat in David's office, coffee mugs in hand. "It's a perfectly legal maneuver," said Wellington. "Not a hint of anything improper, but will Henry use it?"

"That's the million dollar question, isn't it?" David held the paper that Mike had given to him earlier. He looked at it as he held it in his hand. "Will he use it? He wouldn't touch that investigator's report on Washington's termination from Batem, but this…this, I think he might use."

Mike set his cup on the coffee table that sat between him and David. "The only thing that would stop him is some misguided judgment that it might hurt people he really cares for."

"The idea is brilliant. You say Ruth thought of it?" asked Bob.

"Yep, can you believe it? The idea was there just waiting for someone to come up with it, and Ruth remembered something Lisa said when we were at dinner; then she called me, we met, and she laid it on me. I called Mike and the rest you know. Mike got the job done. Well, let's just hope Henry will use it and that it will have the effect we think it will."

Bob and Mike rose to leave. Mike made it clear he'd be back around 3:30 to sweat it out with David and the others. Bob Wellington couldn't be there because he would be a part of the board meeting, as the company's legal counsel and a longtime director. David and Bob shook hands; they squeezed each other a little more firmly than usual. Mike laid his hand on Bob's shoulder, "Will we see you before you go into the meeting?"

"Probably not, I've still got some last minute details to take care of."

"Well, good luck," Mike said as he patted Bob's shoulder.

"Ditto," said David. Bob looked at them both, almost said something, but instead he shook his head affirmatively, squared his shoulders, and left them with a wink. This big hunk of a guy who always had a wry or comical comment was someone you would want in your corner when push came to shove. David and Mike were glad Bob Wellington would be at the board meeting this afternoon. They felt certain it would be a comfort to the boss.

CHAPTER 44

Sitting at his desk, Henry turned in his chair looking out the window at the miniature world below him. Seeing the small figures of people and things walking and moving about, he suddenly thought how small his world had gotten— Ruth, the children, ICA. At the moment, ICA occupied most of his thoughts, but he thought of how in the vast universe his problem was infinitesimal, though to him it was all consuming and unrelenting. He stood up, stretched, and walked across the room into the small space between his office and the board room. He sat once more, this time in his aged, but comfortable, recliner. He stared at the wall of pictures in front of him representing years of travel with Ruth, his children, business meetings, conventions and an entire collage of personal and business momentos. Good times, he thought, as he reviewed the smorgasbord of impressions ranging from him and Ruth meeting Golda Meir in Israel, many years earlier, to a visit with his daughter on a kibbutz. Then there was the stunning sunset in the background as Ruth leaned against a rock on a trip to the Grand Canyon shortly after their marriage. God, she was beautiful, he thought. There was Palms Springs and a picture of David and himself with several general agents and producers at the Boulders just outside of Scottsdale on a day of golf. As he glanced farther down the wall a favorite moment of his had been captured on film. Henry was lying in a baggage cart in a train station in Switzerland, mountains in the background, surrounded by nearly one hundred sales associates who were looking at him, smiling and laughing. We put on some great meetings, he thought. We had some great times.

He reached over and took a kleenex from a box on the small table next to him. He blew his nose but also dabbed a tear from his eye. He was feeling not sorry for himself, but melancholy. He continued reminiscing, thinking of the good times, years of loving and being loved. How had it all come to this point, he wondered. Then, he closed his eyes and dozed lightly. It was still early and he had a long day in front of him. More to the point, he had a crucial four o'clock date with his board.

CHAPTER 45

After lunch in the cafeteria, David and Mike called and asked Nancy for a few minutes with Henry. She called David back shortly to say that Henry would see them at 2 P.M., and at exactly that time David and Mike appeared in front of Nancy's desk. As they were walking from the elevator to Henry's suite, they had run into Dick Washington near the men's room. He pointed towards the lavatory and said, "You two should take a close look at the toilet, you'll both be going into it around five o'clock today." Washington grinned at his own attempt at humor. David and Mike glared at him but continued their walk toward Henry's office.

Nancy thought about what last minute business the two men might have with Henry. Probably just wanted to wish him luck, she thought. After shutting the door, David approached Henry's desk, stood in front of it, and, without a word, reached into his pocket, pulled out an envelope, and handed it to Henry who accepted it, opened it, looked at it, and read the contents. His face was that of the great poker player he always was. At out-of-town meetings he would love a good poker game in his suite with those he most closely trusted. Some were home office employees, some were field people, but to be invited to Henry's poker game was an honor; it meant you were trusted not to take advantage of your personal relationship and that Henry enjoyed your company.

After perusing the contents of the envelope, Henry looked at David and Mike and said simply, "Thank you, thank you both." Each shook Henry's hand and whispered, "Good luck."

CHAPTER 46

At five minutes to four on the afternoon of Monday, December 5th, Nancy had the room prepared exactly as she had for each board meeting over the past twenty years. Four times each year she made certain fifteen chairs were placed around the long conference table that could have held up to twice the expected number of participants. Each seat had a legal pad and ICA logoed pen in front of it. A glass also stood in front of each participant's place along with a pitcher of ice water. The pitcher was stainless steel and in sharp contrast to the black mahogany inlaid table on which it stood.

The Board Room itself was very beautiful, not overdone, the long table being the focus of the room. One wall was almost all windows. Looking east, and under the right conditions, one could see Lake Michigan. The opposite wall held a bar, and on a counter stood a coffee urn with all of the accoutrements. On each side of the bar was a succession of pictures, past presidents of ICA and board chairmen. At one end of the room there was an unusual mural stretching from one end of that wall to the other. It started on the left with the company's original home office building and then progressed to the right showing the four buildings ICA had occupied over the years, ending with the present structure. The fourth wall, behind where the chairman sat, held a variety of audiovisual paraphernalia. Just to the right of that was a door leading to the chairman's office. Historically, after all the directors had been seated, the chairman would enter the room through that door. Today at Henry's instructions, Nancy had set two of the fifteen chairs at the head of the table, one for himself and the other for Dick Washington. Henry would still enter through the connecting door. Dick would enter the room with the other directors through the double doors at the center of the wall that also held the bar.

The Board Room carpeting was charcoal gray with a maroon border and it was plush. That carpeting along with special acoustical tiles and insulation in the ceiling and walls made it virtually impossible to hear anything said inside the room from the outside. It also made it possible to hear a whisper inside the room.

Minutes of the last board meeting had been sent out to each

director along with an agenda of today's meeting. Nancy had, however, set out a duplicate copy of both in a file folder in front of each seat. It was one minute to 4 P.M. and the room was now filled with all of ICA's directors, including Richard Washington, who stood in a corner of the room in conversation with Dena Callahan and two others. It was time to call the meeting to order.

CHAPTER 47

Twelve directors sat in their high-backed chairs of maroon leather at the Board Room's table. In the group were Richard Washington, Dena Callahan, and Bob Wellington. The other board members included Barry Hornsfelt, a longtime Henry Rothblatt ally and someone all knew could be counted on to be in Henry's corner during any battle. Bill Lewis, chairman and chief executive officer of a major software company, sat next to Bob Wellington. They were friendly and had known each other for years, but they were in decidedly different camps. Lewis believed in Dick Washington and honestly felt Dick's presentation of the facts was straightforward and an honest assessment of how he felt about the company's overall position. He liked and trusted Henry but wasn't certain about the soundness of his judgment because of his grave illness.

To Lewis' right sat Fred Wileman, chairman of Mountainside Investment and Trust Company. Wileman was an admirer of Henry's for the past seven years, since becoming a board member, but he felt Washington made a compelling case, and Mike and David, at best, considered him neutral. Sitting directly across from Wileman was Terry Rickert, president of the Chicago Bar Association and a fine attorney, though in his grey pinstriped suit and starched white shirt he was, as he appeared, very straight-laced and a bit pompous. He would be on the side of whatever made the most sense to him monetarily. John Hoagg, who sat to the right of Rickert, was absolutely in Washington's camp. Dick had recommended Hoagg five years earlier after the death of a longtime director. Henry was undecided at that time between several candidates, one of whom was Hoagg, chairman and chief financial O\officer of Day Workers, one of the country's largest temporary employment services. Washington gave Hoagg the needed boost. Hoagg would not be likely to forget the favor from Washington. David and Mike were agreed that the other four directors were either solidly aligned with Washington or uncertain. The four had all come on the board within two years of each other.

From 1989 to 1992, there had been four deaths of board members. All agreed that they had never heard of a board losing so many members in such a short period of time. It was a major loss to the company, and Henry spent many long hours and weeks finding the people he felt were the correct replacements for each board member.

Typically, board members are chosen for some special expertise they bring to the table as well as for their general business acumen. Lawrence Porterfield was one of those Henry chose to fill one of the vacancies on his board. He was an easy choice because Porterfield had been recommended by Barry Hornsfelt. Barry's banking business gave him ample opportunity to witness CEO's and chairmen of boards close up. He had alerted Henry to Lawrence Porterfield's potential as a candidate for ICA. He would bring a wealth of business experience and was a bright Harvard graduate who was self-made. As a self-made man, he was a fiercely independent thinker and very focused. He was also active in a number of Chicago philanthropic endeavors and charities. Henry immediately liked Lawrence Porterfield, and it took very little time for him to decide to invite him to participate as an ICA board member. Porterfield accepted and had now served for nearly five years. During that period, his own business had been sold making him immensely wealthy, and he had started a new venture now in its fourth year of operation, and he served as its CEO and chairman. Porterfield Trucking was growing into one of the largest truck rental companies in the country.

At a Chicago Bear–Denver football game in 1991, Henry sat in a skybox at Fred Wileman's invitation. During the half-time ceremonies at the game, Henry accidentally spilled beer on a man he had been introduced to earlier. As he apologized, he feebly attempted to wipe the spots from the man's tweed jacket.

"It's all right. I'm kind of glad you did that. Matter of fact, don't wipe a thing off."

Surprised by the man's response, he said, "But I feel terribly; let me have it cleaned or replaced, please."

The man, much taller and broader than Henry, replied, "Look, my wife gave me this jacket for my birthday two years ago. I really don't like it at all, but I have to wear it occasionally or hurt her feelings. This will be a good excuse to get rid of it."

"But won't she want to have it cleaned?" asked an amused Henry

Rothblatt.

The man reached for Henry's beer cup and Henry handed it to him. Then, to Henry's astonishment, the man poured the balance of Henry's beer all over his jacket which he now held in one hand. "Now she won't; she hates the smell of stale beer."

The two men laughed and thus Henry had met Kevin McDougal whom he promptly invited to lunch during the week. It turned out that Kevin was the president and chief executive of McDougal Fasteners, manufacturers of all sorts of devices that held things together, from staples to pins. Although McDougal had inherited the business from his father, he had taken the company public some years earlier, and it was the darling of the NASDAQ for a few years. More recently, it had traded in a fairly tight range, but the company racked up profits year after year.

Within a year of their chance meeting, Kevin McDougal had been invited to sit on ICA's board. Henry found him to be astute and aggressive and extremely inquisitive. A very good choice; not afraid to ask questions. Kevin and Henry had great respect for one another, though their management styles were miles apart—Henry, conservative and thoughtful, Kevin, bold and aggressive, much more impulsive. Both, however, shared the skills of asking questions and both were exceptionally good listeners.

In the corner of the room, opposite from where Dena and Washington were conferring, stood George Walke. Walke was one of the board's newest members, having been appointed about three years earlier. Although Henry had selected him to sit on his board, he probably knew less about George than most of his other directors, whom he felt he knew pretty well. Since joining the ICA board, Walke pretty much stayed to himself. In the travel business, he had written several books on the subject of travel and had built an internet travel empire. He took his site in the opposite direction from most of the discounters. TRAVEL GOOD had been built on upscale travel adventures with attention paid to detail, value, and communication, but not price. For the upscale traveler, TRAVEL GOOD was the place to get information and to book the vacation of a lifetime. George Walke was self-made, a loner but bright, and one of those rarities, a person who is knowledgeable about nearly everything. All Henry really knew about his private life was that he was extremely well read. George Walke had been brought to Henry's attention by an acquaintance of Ruth's and actually met him for the first time at a bridge game they had been invited to. George and his wife were marvelous bridge players, and Ruth and Henry thoroughly enjoyed playing with them. Over the period of a couple of years, Henry admired George's bridge skills and allowed him to arrange a couple of interesting vacations for him and Ruth. TRAVEL GOOD did a marvelous job, and Henry thought it was a wonderfully run company. In addition, Henry liked what he had learned from George and from many others who had only great things to say about this articulate and interesting individual.

CHAPTER 48

In March 1992, the last of the three men who died in a short span of years passed away. He was replaced by Myron Gold

On the evening before the December board meeting, David and Mike sat with the newest director having convinced him to have dinner at Henry's request, though Henry would not be present.

Sitting in a downtown restaurant where they had decided to meet, David and Mike had arrived first. "Have you heard anything from anyone else that we've met with?" asked David.

"Nope, not a single word, but then, you know what they say, no news is..."

"Maybe not in this case," snapped David.

"Listen, we've done our best with the ammunition we've been given, David."

A short stocky mustached fellow approached and smiled. He stuck his hand out to David and said, " Hello, David." David smiled right back, took and shook the man's hand, and held out his palm to have a seat at their table.

"Good to see you, Myron. You know Mike, I believe?" Myron, nattily dressed in a black cashmere sportcoat and tan slacks, looked at Mike, stuck his hand out again, and shook it. "I don't recall having the pleasure of meeting Mike before, but David and I are old friends. Met at our tailor's a time or two."

David smiled, "How are you, Myron?" Myron Gold, average size, average looking, except for the way he dressed, but with huge hands. A plumber's apprentice turned plumber, turned owner of one of the largest plumbing supply companies in the country, also one of the shrewdest businessmen Henry had ever met.

After a few minutes of chat about local politics and the prospects for the Bulls for the rest of the season, David slowly began a three-step process. As they were finishing their first round of drinks, he introduced the subject matter they had gathered to discuss. Because he had told Myron that Henry had asked him and Mike to visit with them, Gold pretty much knew what the topic of the evening was going to be.

David and Mike's meetings with some of the Board directors had not gone particularly well. It was a foregone conclusion that Bill Lewis and John Hoagg would vote with Washington, and Henry, David, and Mike also reluctantly put Rickert in the Washington camp.

Naturally, Bob Wellington and Barry Hornsfeldt could be counted upon, but that was really it. The man they were meeting with tonight could hold the key. Since Henry could not vote as chairman, but Washington could cast a ballot as the interim chairperson, they seemed to face a very close, or even losing, vote. Henry could cast a ballot in the event the vote were tied, however. The way David and Mike had it forecasted was that Hornsfeldt and Wellington were the only sure votes. Wileman was a toss-up along with Rickert and Myron Gold. Rickert and Gold were the key to any decision. If they could capture their votes, then Henry could perhaps cast the deciding ballot. They needed the vote of Gold, and, in addition, had to convince either Wileman or Rickert to cast their ballot for Corey. There was little chance of convincing some of the others to change their minds, at least that was their thinking .

To be sure, all of the board members saw dollar signs dancing in front of their eyes. Even Barry Hornsfeldt and Bob Wellington would admit to that, but it was a question, as Henry put it, of doing the right thing. Gold was about to hear what the right thing was and why.

Thus the second step of David's mission was to present Mike Spellari as something of an expert in the matter and someone who had all of Henry's confidence. As Mike listened to David talk with Gold, he marveled at his smooth delivery and convincing attitude. For Mike it was easy. He was certain that following Henry Rothblatt would be the right thing to do.

CHAPTER 49

During the two-and-one-half-hour dinner, Mike elaborated on the four reasons why the status quo ought to be maintained for the benefit of ICA, the policyholders, ICA employees, and the Field. Mike completed his presentation with a passionate plea for Myron's vote. He made certain he understood that the vote was not simply for a new president of ICA, but would determine the future direction of the company and whether it would turn into an IPO situation.

At that point, David left the table for a moment and returned with Corey Topping in hand. Corey had been waiting in the bar for over an hour so that he could join them and answer any questions Gold might have for him. Those questions took up yet another hour, and when Gold had left, Corey Topping looked at an exhausted Mike Spellari and said, "What do you think?"

"I think you, Corey, were awesome." David shook Corey's hand as he continued, "Mike was spectacular, and.....I don't honestly know what he's thinking or how he'll vote, but both of you guys were just spectacular." David had turned his head toward no one in particular, "God damn it, God damn it..." It wasn't exactly a cry, but it wasn't far from it.

CHAPTER 50

As the board settled into their seats, Nancy sat next to an empty chair near the head of the table. Her chair was backed up just enough so anyone would realize she was not a board member. This was truly not necessary, but it was sort of a tradition. She was there to take notes, assisting Bob Wellington who acted as the board's secretary and keeper of the minutes of each meeting. Nancy Wagner also was there to help and assist the man who had headed ICA for the past twenty years as president and chairman of this board, the man who now stood in the frame of the doorway that connected his office to the Board Room. As they all looked up in that direction, they saw he was still the tall wiry figure he had always been though he was bony thin now with skin that was pasty and very pale. Each of them could see that the medication, radiation, and other treatments, as well as the cancer itself, had taken its toll. Henry was a bit unsteady as he walked slowly to his seat next to Washington. He stood at his leather chair holding onto the top of it with his left hand and shaking hands with the other. One by one each of the men present, with the exception of Washington and the one female board member, walked over to Henry, shook his hand, and uttered a few words of greeting or encouragement. This was true even of those lined up to vote against him. They came to him out of genuine concern yet some of them wondered about his ability to see the issues clearly. After all, they reasoned, how clear could his thinking be if only because of the medications he was on?

Now it was time for battle. Henry said one last silent prayer for strength. The board took their seats and Dick Washington began to speak. "As your vice chairman, and at Henry's suggestion, I will chair today's meeting."

A few eyebrows were raised. Henry had every right to chair this meeting and thus gain some measure of control. The pervasive thinking in the room at that moment was that he just didn't have the physical strength to do so, yet at that precise moment Henry felt pretty good. He had rested all day in his office suite and his adrenaline was flowing. He involuntarily touched his coat pocket to check on the envelope he carried there.

Dick Washington asked for a reading of the minutes from ICA's last board meeting. As Bob Wellington began to read them, he glanced at Henry and saw that he was alert and attentive. Bob Wellington then did his job and read the minutes to a board that was somewhat less than interested. The battle, that's what they were interested in, the battle of wills between a cunning and ruthless Richard Washington and the crafty veteran of the wars, Henry Rothblatt.

CHAPTER 51

As Bob Wellington was about to ask for approval of the reading of the minutes, downstairs in David's office sat Mike Spellari and Jerry Barton.

"Think they've gotten to it yet?" asked Barton.

Mike laughed, "Jerry, I don't think they've even started the meeting. It was called for 4 o'clock, all those directors will bullshit for half an hour before they even read the minutes. To justify their presence, each one will probably have a little something to say. Then they'll get to old business and no doubt start discussing some crap that has nothing to do with anything, and then, finally, new business. That should be around 10 tonight."

"You're kidding, of course," remarked Barton and both David and Mike gave a too loud, nervous laugh.

"This tension and waiting is killing me," David said, as he took a seat opposite Jerry and Mike with a glass, triangular-shaped coffee table between them. They were all tense and edgy, but it would be a couple of hours, at least, before they knew anything. In the meantime, Corey waited in his office to be called for his interview by the entire board. The phone rang and David jumped up to answer, while the other men's eyes were glued to his quickly moving form. Grabbing the phone he said in a shrill voice, "David Rourke."

"Any news?" It was Lisa.

"Oh hi, sweetheart, nothing yet. It'll be quite awhile. I'll call as soon as I know anything, okay?"

"David, I love that man. I'm praying for him…..for all of you."

"I know, honey, we've done everything we can; we all love him. It's out of our hands now. I'll call you as soon as we learn anything. Love you."

CHAPTER 52

The minutes having been read and approved, virtually without comment, Dick Washington proceeded to old business. While there was plenty they could have discussed, again, there were only a few meaningless statements or questions.

Good, Washington thought. They want to get to it. To him that meant getting rid of Henry and getting on with self-enrichment and self-engrandisement. He was positive the mood of the board was perfect for the occasion.

"New business?" There was silence in the room and it was stifling, thought Wellington. It was only 4:15 and they were already at new business. This was a first for this board, he thought. It was a first for any board he had ever been a part of.

Dena had similar thoughts; dressed in her navy blue dress, buttoned to her neck, she was the picture of conservatism and propriety. She glanced up at Richard and thought she saw a tremor at the corner of his mouth, then thought it might have been a slight smile that he decided to hide at the last moment. In any event, she also was anxious to get on with it. Visions of a yacht sailing in the Caribbean danced in her head.

"Our agenda under new business calls for the election of a president to succeed Henry who, as we all know, would like to retire. The process this afternoon will be to hear from anyone who wishes to nominate a candidate and then ask for seconds. Once we have all the nominations, we'll ask the candidates to address the board. We've all met with these individuals prior to this meeting so this simply allows for last minute questions of them prior to this very important vote."

Washington appeared eager to continue. "I'll now ask"... suddenly there was an interruption.

"Mr. Vice-Chairman," Bob Wellington rose from his chair as he spoke. "Mr. Vice-Chairman, I'm certain it was an oversight, but of course anyone nominating or seconding a candidate is also entitled to speak in favor of their candidate."

"Yes, Bob, thank you, of course. As Bob has correctly pointed out, anyone who nominates or seconds a nomination may, if they

162

wish, say a few words on behalf of their candidate."

"Mr. Vice-Chairman," said Wellington, "our bylaws do not say that those who nominate or those who second must speak necessarily about the candidate nor, by the way, do they make any reference to a few words or any other time limit."

Washington, clearly annoyed now, responded with babble. "Yes, I realize that, I thought, I mean, well, let's just get on with it, shall we?" Washington sitting now, ruffled through papers in front of him clearly trying to collect his thoughts. Dena wondered what the point was to Wellington's remarks.

"Mr. Wellington, this chair has no intention of short-cutting or depriving the process of its full due. However, your remarks prompt me to offer to relinquish this chair during the election process to a member of the board, any member at all."

"That won't be necessary," Henry said as he stood at his chair. "You're doing just fine, please continue," and then Henry sat. He had said little, yet Barry Hornsfelt thought to himself, the son of a bitch is regal, like a king. Goddamn, Henry, right on.

"The chair," said Washington, "asks for nominations for the presidency of Insurance Company of America."

As though on cue, Dena announced, "Mr. Chairman, I wish to place in nomination, the name of our vice-chairman, Richard Washington."

"Temporary vice chair," quickly added Bob Wellington.

"Yes," said Dena caustically, "temporary vice chairman." Richard Washington now called for seconds. They came quickly from John Hoagg and Bill Lewis. Neither man, however, added anything other than simply saying "second."

No longer any doubt about Bill Lewis' loyalties, thought Bob.

"Thank you," Washington perfunctorily responded.

Bob Wellington now stood behind his chair and in a firm voice said, "I am honored to place in nomination the name of Corey Topping for the presidency of ICA." Bob of course knew that whoever secured the presidency of ICA would, in all likelihood, within a brief period of time, be named as chairman of this very board of directors. The waiting period was a check to make certain of the fitness of the man to the company.

Bob also knew that the members of this board were well aware they were voting on an even larger issue than who would be the president of the company. They understood that each candidate had a specific agenda. Corey Topping would be in favor of the status quo, keeping ICA a life insurance company that continued to be owned and operated for the benefit of the policyholders.

Richard Washington, if elected, would create a public company out of ICA, and it would operate primarily for the benefit of its stockholders. Washington would make certain that he and his cronies, man and woman, would be stockholders and they would acquire their interest under very favorable terms. Those sitting around the conference table understood that Henry's personal endorsement of Corey Topping was a statement of his extreme interest and prejudice in this whole matter. Corey's second came from Fred Wileman. Wellington looked up in surprise. Maybe there was at least a glimmer of hope. He hadn't known what to expect from Wileman. Barry Hornsfelt provided another second to the nomination; nothing unusual in that.

"Any other nominations?" After a brief silence, Washington continued, "There being none, we will proceed. Each candidate may be interviewed for up to an hour by the board. This will provide us with yet another opportunity to hear from each of them before a vote is called for. Each nominator may speak on behalf of their candidate as may those who seconded the nominations. Well, let's get started. The chair will submit himself first for any questions."

This had been a decision that Washington and Dena had thought long and hard about. In the end, they felt Corey would not be able to stand up to Washington's charisma and his story.

"Who would like to start? I stand prepared to answer any and all of your questions."

John Hoagg asked, "Richard, why don't you tell us your vision of the future for ICA."

Remaining seated, Washington straightened his tie, cleared his throat, and began, "Thank you, John. Before I start, let me say that all of us at ICA owe an enormous debt of gratitude to Henry Rothblatt for guiding this company to its present position. Whatever our differences in point of view, we certainly cannot deny the enormously important groundwork that Henry has laid for us, building the infrastructure of what is today a great company." As he spoke, he glanced at Henry. He was certain he could detect Henry working to hide his distaste of him; undeterred, he continued.

"Companies, however, plateau; they get stale. I believe our company falls into that category. All around us companies from every industry are searching to grow, to acquire, or to merge. Companies are looking to diversify. On that count, we are reasonably well situated. But my feeling is we must also grow through creative acquisition."

As he went on, Henry could tell that Washington was being listened to. Even those he knew to be his allies looked as though they were somewhat mesmerized by Washington's words, and the forceful and competent manner in which he delivered them were undeniably appealing.

"ICA is still in the dark ages economically and financially. The company is going to make money virtually in spite of anything we do. It would take nothing less than a catastrophic event to dent our balance sheet. But, we are not capitalizing on our assets, using them to their fullest potential."

As he went on more than a few on the board were ready to fire questions his way, but he steam-rolled ahead without leaving an inch for them to say a word. "We are a cash rich company, yes, but we must prepare to access the capital markets in order to be in a position to borrow, if necessary, when the right acquisition opportunity comes along. We must process money more efficiently and quickly, and we are way behind the curve technologically. ICA presently does not conduct its business in a modern, efficient, strategic manner. In short, the bottom line is at the bottom of this company's list of priorities. Interpersonal relationships and something euphemistically referred to as our corporate culture seems more important and gets more attention than do our financial results."

Richard was warming to the task and Dena knew there was a risk that he might go too far. Board members did not want to see Henry,

ICA, or Henry's past contributions denigrated in any way. At the other end of the table Bob Wellington looked directly at Henry to check for a reaction, but he need not have been concerned. Henry sat, his chair set back from the table slightly, legs crossed, hands folded neatly in his lap, his expression giving no hint of how he felt about Washington's oratory. Bob Wellington thought to himself that he didn't know if Henry could bear a continuation of the company-bashing that Dick Washington seemed to be engaged in. The company that Henry was such a force in, that he so loved, was not at all the company Washington was describing. But Henry sat almost stoically and continued to listen as Richard went on.

"At the pleasure of the board, this company can be operated profitably in one of two ways. First, it can be operated as a cash cow. We simply become experts at maintaining our business as it is. We could reduce expenses drastically and, in fact, from what I've witnessed, expense ratios could be improved at least 25 percent. We would only need to market and sell enough new products to replace what we lose through natural attrition. In turn, that strategy relieves us of the enormous investment we make each year in attracting new business. As it stands now, it takes at least three to four years for us, not to make money, but just to break even on the sale of a new life insurance policy. Why? Why should we do that? We could just ride the wave and have our cash cow for the rest of our lifetimes and well beyond, but if that's our choice, we must begin to position ourselves.

"The alternative would be to position ourselves to access the capital markets so that we could grow ICA through acquisition and expansion. As you all know, I've been working with our esteemed colleague and fellow director, Dena Callahan. I've asked her to share some research and thoughts we have on this second, and frankly, preferred option. Dena?"

In all of her glory, Dena stood before the board of ICA and for the next fifteen minutes held most of them spellbound with her presentation. More than one man wondered if he was more caught up in what she was saying or the way she looked, which was actually quite stunning though businesslike. After passing the usual charts and graphs around the table, her presentation finished and she returned to her chair. She had done the university and herself quite proud.

Henry seemed unperturbed and barely glanced at any of the material that had been placed in front of him. He had already made up his mind to go in a substantially different direction.

Washington now stood and asked for questions. Bob Wellington actually had several he wanted to pose, but previously he and Henry had decided to hold their questions which would limit the amount of propaganda Washington could spread. After a few inquiries of a mostly perfunctory nature from other of the board's members, Richard Washington, broad smile on his face, called for Corey Topping to take his turn before the directors. Since Corey was not a board member, he was not in the room and Nancy would have to call his office, which had been previously arranged. It would take a few minutes for Corey to appear. This was an opportunity to break and they were told they would reassemble in fifteen minutes.

CHAPTER 53

It was now over an hour since the board had first been drawn together, and in David's office several people had gathered. They passed the time, first discussing the possible outcome of the board's decision, and then the range of consequences of that decision. Eventually, the conversation began to address a number of wide-ranging issues, and at the moment managed healthcare had their attention. David sat behind his desk and stared into space, his mind a million miles away. He hoped they would hear something soon; he had no patience and the waiting was excruciating.

David's mind drifted and the conversation of the others muted in the background. Suddenly he was in Monterey, California. It was 1987. David had been in the Home Office for just a couple of years when he ran a regional meeting for the company. All of ICA's agents from west of the Rockies were in attendance. On the first day of the meeting, the agenda called for David to address about one thousand agents, welcome them, discuss the meeting agenda, and extol the virtues of an agent's role with the company. Since this was his first major address to a large group of agents, he was understandably nervous. As he walked toward the stage and podium on the first morning of the program, he found his breath coming in short gasps as he realized that the talk he had painstakingly prepared was not in his pocket. It was not in his pocket, briefcase or in his room, he knew, for it dawned on him that he had absentmindedly thrown it in a wastecan with his morning paper after breakfast. Sweat started pouring from his forehead and under his arms. Usually speaking to a crowd didn't particularly bother him, but at that moment, he could not recall one word of what he had wanted to say. There he stood in front of all those people, including his fellow Home Office staff and his boss, Henry Rothblatt, and he could not think of one word to utter.

His hands gripped the side of the podium, his shirt was drenched under the suit coat he had so laboriously selected to wear, and Henry Rothblatt and one thousand others awaited his presentation.

Someone called his name. Who was that? Where are you? David opened his eyes and looked about.

"David, honey, I didn't mean to startle you."

"Lisa?"

"Honey, what's wrong? You look awful; are you okay?"

"Oh, sure, absolutely. I was just daydreaming."

David straightened himself, smoothed his tie, and ran his hand through his hair. Lisa touched his cheek with her hand and at once he knew she understood.

David couldn't help returning to his "daydream" which, in fact, actually happened. He knew exactly why his mind had conjured up the images of what had occurred. It had been the first time he had thought of Henry as a mentor. Henry had dismissed the incident almost without mention that day. David had been mortally embarrassed. It seemed to him that he had stood at that podium interminably and, in fact, it had been for quite a while. After he had finally composed himself, he had done a rather admirable job of making his presentation right off the top of his head.

After dinner Henry had asked David to have a drink in his suite. Once they were relaxed, Henry, who sat directly across from David, reached across and put his hand on David's knee. "God, I remember the first time I got stage fright," he had said. "Lot bigger crowd too and not so friendly. Ruth had to bolster my self-esteem for weeks."

"Really?" David asked.

"Absolutely. I've never been so petrified before or since. It was a group of company officers from around the country, nearly 1,500 of them as I recall. Good Lord, I thought I'd never be able to look at any of them again. Then a good friend who was at the meeting told me the same thing had happened to him and we realized it had probably happened at one time or another to anyone who is in that position with any frequency. Your episode just happened to be your first time out, that's all." David immediately felt better about himself. Just knowing that Henry and others of similar stature had gone through the same situation was comforting.

Some months later David had reason to stop in to see Henry, who had not yet arrived home. Ruth and he were chatting about one thing and another when David had occasion to relate what had happened to him, including Henry's response. He thought Ruth's face looked puzzled and he quickly realized that nothing of the sort had ever happened to Henry. It was simply Henry's ruse to put David at ease. When Henry arrived home that evening, he greeted David. They completed their business and after Henry shook his hand and said goodbye, David turned, looked at him and said, "You're a rascal."

"What?"

"You're a rascal."

"Why do you say that?"

"Ask Ruth."

CHAPTER 54

After reconvening, and with everyone seated, Washington gave a nondescript introduction to Corey Topping. The young man, younger looking even than his actual age, was now standing before the group waiting his turn to speak and answer questions. With salt and pepper hair and a very slight build, he was short, which added to his youthful look. David and Mike had wondered to each other if his look was a bit napoleanic. They had decided, however, that the moment Corey spoke everyone would know this was a great guy whose appearance belied his deep knowledge along with his business and street smarts. When Washington finished his introduction, Corey laid a folder on the table in front of him and drew his glasses off. His suit was loose on his short but athletic frame. His wife had put him on a strict diet months earlier and all his clothes were too big. It didn't bother him in the least. He stood very close to Henry and placed a hand on his shoulder as he began to speak.

"Henry Rothblatt is my dear friend, my boss, my mentor. For fourteen of the twenty years Henry has been at the helm of this company, I have stood alongside him, I've learned from him. I like Henry Rothblatt; I like our company and I like what I've learned. Most of you know that, like Henry, I'm an actuary by both education and practice, but I'm a different kind of actuary, and I think that's because I've learned from a different kind of actuary."

Corey paused and looked down at Henry, then removed his hand from his shoulder and squared himself to the room full of ICA directors. He pulled himself to his full height, which was only about five feet, ten inches, and went on. "Many would tell you that actuaries are people who are always looking out the back window of the car to see where they've been. I've learned the importance of keeping my eyes peeled out the front window as well, so I can keep my focus on where I want to go. We're entering an environment that is going to take careful navigation through dangerous and, in some cases, uncharted waters. It will pay to depend on experience but it will be critical to have a vision. This vision must be clear and flexible, and a knowledge of this business and industry will be mandatory."

At that, Richard Washington moved in his chair and put a look on his face that said hogwash, but he sat silently and continued to listen to the young Mr. Topping. "Henry Rothblatt may be an actuary but he is a great leader and visionary as well. It is very difficult to market the products we sell. Think about how many calls each of you receive weekly from people you don't know, and probably some whom you do know, asking if they can speak with you about your insurance, investments, or your company's employees benefits." That seemed to strike a chord and several of the board smiled in recognition or grumbled under their breath.

"It's been said that people work for money and for a leader. Henry has been that leader. Our field force, our sales force, is the very best in the industry. We have excellent retention of our sales people because, among other reasons, they know, respect, and admire Henry Rothblatt...they are working for a leader. The same could be said about the retention of our company's employees. Our people are experienced and the knowledge runs deep because we don't lose people. They too have bought into the culture that Henry has created and crafted so well. The leadership he's provided has inspired many, and it is built on doing what is right. Do the right thing for all of your constituencies, the policyholders, the field, the company's employees. Avoid the fast buck ideas, avoid the schemes, keep the company strong financially and keep risks to minimal levels. I have grown up at his feet and I feel exactly the same way Henry does about those things. A life insurance policy is a contract, a promise to pay. To meet our obligations we must remain fiscally conservative."

Corey could sense he was on a small roll and began to slowly circle the table stopping at each Director's chair and addressing his remarks to each of them, looking them in the eye as he spoke. "There are those who may misunderstand the purpose or the mission of a mutual life insurance company. They might misunderstand to the extent that they think of this company as their own. Make no mistake, it isn't my company, your company, or *their* company. We are simply the custodians of ICA, for its real, true, rightful owners, and they are each of ICA's policyholders. Looking at it in that light, this board is faced with a clear choice. Name as its chief executive officer an individual who has made no secret of his ambition to take ICA down a new road, a new course, or you can select the candidate that Henry Rothblatt, the individual most responsible for ICA's respected and strong position today, has decided to propose. I can see where it might be possible for a lay person to draw the wrong conclusions about a direction for this company, but the choice to me is very clear. Henry feels I'm the best person to keep ICA on its present course. Understand, as Henry does, there will probably be changes if you see fit to give me the opportunity. But, the changes will be to enhance the company's present mission. The changes will be directed at keeping us in the position of being the best possible custodians of the privilege of serving our clients and real owners. We will always reassess risk and stay modern and contemporary but we will not do anything to jeopardize the ability of ICA to keep its promises. Nor will we do anything that would wrest ownership from where it properly belongs."

As Corey completed his walk around the table he came to a standstill in back of Henry's chair. "The executive management of this company is totally dedicated to our owners and to this board; all of us hope you feel the same toward us. Give us our company, and we'll make this an institution you will be very proud of and proud to be a part of. I realize I haven't great visibility with this board, but you do know Henry Rothblatt. My lack of visibility with the board was a function of what my role has been, namely, to be a team player and learn from the master. I've done both and I'm ready for this opportunity. I greatly appreciate your consideration and your time. Thank you."

As Corey finished, Henry turned and grasped one of his hands and squeezed; he looked up and gave an affirmative smile. Clearly he was proud of Corey whom he considered one of his protégés. Corey turned and left the room as Henry was looking for a palpable pulse to be felt or read. Superb as he had been, Henry doubted Corey had changed anyone's mind, but then he just couldn't tell.

Fred Wileman stood and looked at his fellow board members. "It seems we have, as Mr. Topping correctly pointed out, a clear choice. I agree, but what about the right choice. I'd like to hear from you,

Henry." Fred looked at Henry, his facial features softened, and his voice lowered as he asked, "Are you up to it, old chap?"

It was now so still in the room that the proverbial pin could have dropped and it would have sounded like a cymbal crashing. All eyes in the room turned toward Henry. Richard and Dena gave each other a knowing look as if to say, well, we expected him to say something. Their feeling was that they had lobbied well and politicked to perfection. Though they might grudgingly admit that Corey Topping had done an excellent job of presenting himself and Henry's position, they also felt that it was much too little, too late. The board knew Corey from their previous one-on-one interviews with him. They also knew Washington, and many of them were absorbed by the pictures of personal gain for each of them that Richard had painted. No, Dena and Richard were not in the least bit concerned.

So, it was finally time for the board to hear directly from Henry. In reality, that's all that was left before a vote. Bob Wellington and Barry Hornsfelt walked over to Henry's place at the table and wished him luck. Washington simply said, "Henry, I believe it's your floor."

Henry sat still for a moment, and then cautiously rose to his feet. He braced himself and stood erect as he faced his board. Yes, his board...he reminded himself that these men and women were still his board. To the familiar eye, he looked both much the same and at the same time very different. The tan had faded, the thinning hair was grayer, the face showed a substantial increase of wrinkles. Yet, it was still the familiar erect posture and square shoulders. When you looked at Henry Rothblatt, the picture screamed of integrity. It did before and it did now. There in the winter's sunlight streaming through the windows, Henry appeared backlit and as an almost spiritual embodiment of righteousness.

Finally he spoke: "To say that I am bitterly disappointed that we have come to this point would be a gross understatement. I've run ICA in a manner of which I am very proud, and why not? This company's record of achievement is enormous and we, you and I, and all of our associates here in the Home Office and in the field have set an example that others could follow, an example of how to build an organization that benefits all. Certainly our policyholders voice no

174

complaints. Through our mutuality we have treated them extremely well; we've been entrusted with their funds and managed them in exemplary fashion. We have built a strong, solid enterprise, and I apologize to no one for doing so in an honorable manner. We have done it with integrity and yes, with honor. At the same time we've built a corporate culture of which we should be proud.

"I'm also really very proud of my candidate for the office of president of ICA who has appeared before you this afternoon. As Corey said, we do what is right. We keep in mind we are not here to speculate with funds given to our trust. Our role is to preserve. We must preserve, not risk. We must always be able to fulfill our promise to pay. Widows and small children, retirees and those on disability are counting on us. The families and businesses we serve require that we remain strong and intact."

Henry seemed to gain a bit of momentum. "This strategy wasn't created by me, and it isn't new. The men who have preceded me for the past 120 years have perpetuated this thinking rather successfully, I would say. Mr. Washington has been a member of the board for nearly ten years. With four board meetings annually, he would have attended approximately forty ICA board meetings. As far as I know, that has been his total involvement with our company and this industry. Of course, he has also had the past two months or so of more or less full-time involvement with our company as my appointed interim vice-chair and temporary CEO. That's it; that's his full range of life insurance industry involvement. What he knows, he has learned here, and I'm afraid he has not learned too well.

"Based on the company's 120 year history, knowledge gained by me from nearly forty years with ICA, and Corey Topping's twenty years of service and involvement, Mr. Washington has totally failed to comprehend what ICA is all about. He compares us to other industries and companies. That is the fatal flaw in his thinking, because we are unlike any other industry or company. Other companies have investors, and the investors know of the risks involved in owning stock. Our policyholders are not aware of any such risk; instead they know of guarantees. They are guaranteed that their families and businesses will survive with the discounted dollars we will deliver to their heirs and beneficiaries. They are depending on our keeping our promises. Mr. Washington would have us change philosophically and speculate to some degree with our clients' money to achieve a possibly greater return. What will this greater return gain? How much greater a return will it be? What will happen to that greater return? Where will it wind up? In the pockets of your policyowners? I would speculate not."

Henry's steel blue eyes now looked directly at Dick Washington who after a few seconds, looked away. "What will we accomplish, Dick, an extra 2 percent or 3 percent? How much additional risk will be forced upon our policyholders, and what will occur if you make a few wrong guesses?" Henry now left the side of his chair where he had stood and began to slowly circle the room, looking over his shoulder, eyes fixed on Dick Washington. "The commercial real estate market offered extraordinary returns in the early eighties; would you have had us invest there? ICA didn't go there to any extent; companies who did, Mutual Benefit Life, for example, didn't fair too well. In case you didn't know, they were forced into receivership. They were a 140-year-old mutual company whose board thought they could outperform those of us who stuck to our guns."

As Henry glanced around the table he did not detect any sign of making a dent in the thinking of those board members lined up against him, much less in the thinking of Dick Washington or Dena Callahan. Still he continued on.

"Maybe junk bonds would suit you better and maybe we could join our brethren such as Executive Life Insurance Company in bankruptcy. That wouldn't be too good for you, Dick. It would mean that the insurance commission would be our new CEO and chairman. For God's sake," the tone and volume of his voice went up a few notches as he turned his gaze back to the board at large, "it's been tried and found wanting. We are not like other companies; we are a life insurance company. Don't let your thinking blur; focus on our purpose. Our purpose and your purpose as directors is to make certain that ICA can back the promises it makes."

Henry stopped; he was back at his chair, standing, and once more looked around the table slowly. Some of the board looked back but most let their eyes drift. A few were busy making notes but most sat hands folded in their laps. Henry could not read them. He really did not want to read them. What they were thinking, at this moment, he felt he didn't want to know. Slowly, exhausted as the adrenalin began to fade, he slipped back into his chair, head slightly bowed. He had given it his best shot, and intuitively felt he'd come up short.

After a few moments of quiet, Dick Washington asked sarcastically, "Gentlemen and ladies, are there any questions of Mr. Rothblatt?" No hands were raised. Bob Wellington could have asked a couple of Henry to help expand his thoughts, but he was afraid Henry wouldn't have the strength. With no questions forthcoming, Washington spoke hesitatingly realizing that though he and Dena had done a good job of privately lobbying and explaining to this group, he did not want to tempt fate. "If there are no more questions or comments..."

"I have a comment or two," Bob Wellington stood up. "I've been around here for over thirty years; I've watched this company grow as I've grown." He put the palms of his hands on his round middle gut and there were a few chuckles. Even Henry managed an amused smile. "No one knows better the condition of this company, and no one understands what is good for this company the way Henry Rothblatt does. What he has told you here this afternoon is the way it really is; you mustn't let your personal agendas get in the way of the right thing to do. The right thing to do is to protect our policyholders at all costs. I fail to see how demutualization, which takes this company away from them, does that. I can see many reasons for going public, none of them involve our policyholders' interest. Mr. Washington, you, sir, are a damn fool."

Before Bob could continue, Washington rose and slapped his hand on the table. "Don't you dare speak to me that way, you, of all people. You couldn't keep an Eskimo out of jail for heating his igloo."

"Maybe not, but I can cost you and this board a lot of money and a lot of sleep, and I'll do just that." Bob turned to face the board members as a whole. "If you're stupid enough to vote this evil, conniving bastard to the office of president of my company…" Bob was pointing a finger at Washington now while standing and fuming with anger. "I'll personally lead a class action suit by our policy-holders against you. I swear!"

"Oh shut up, Wellington, and sit down. You won't lead anything against anyone. You'll take your pension and roll your fat ass back and forward in a hammock in the yard. You won't allow anything to disturb your precious pension plan."

Before Bob could bark back, Henry held up his hand and asked for quiet. "Bob, relax, sit, my friend. Dick, you sit down too." Washington found himself obeying Henry as Bob Wellington had done. Bob obeyed out of force of habit and respect. Washington obeyed and, at that moment, could have not told you why he did so. Dena Callahan who was thinking about what her role might be in this debate, suddenly found herself just looking to see what Henry was going to say or do next. The others pretty much followed Dena's lead and found themselves looking at Henry as if for advice. It had always been this way. Henry Rothblatt didn't need to raise his voice or gesticulate to command attention. His charisma, even now, in a weakened state, was overpowering.

Henry sighed and said, "My board has always conducted itself with dignity, respect, and decorum; it will continue to do so for the little time I have left as its chairman. Mr. Vice-Chairman, this is still your meeting to conduct. I believe you were about to ask for a vote on the presidency of ICA in the absence of further questions or comments, but I have a request if I may?"

The bewildered Richard Washington stared back at Henry not realizing he needed to reply to him; finally, after a pregnant pause, he respond, "Thank you, Henry. Yes, yes, you have a request?"

"Mr. Vice-Chairman, and gentlemen of the board, I would like to ask for a straw vote, a non-binding vote just to see where everyone stands."

"I see no reason why this board could not accommodate your request, Henry, though I feel the vote should be closed. You can each write the name of Corey Topping or myself on a slip of notepaper, fold it, and pass it to Mr. Wellington, our secretary. Mr. Wellington will count and announce the vote, which I remind you is non-binding."

"Thank you," responded Henry.

After writing a name on a piece of notepaper, each member passed his or her vote to Bob Wellington who, after a slow counting, announced four votes for Corey Topping, eight for Richard Washington. Henry was not at all surprised. He looked around the table and could tell how each of them had voted. Even if he could not have guessed, he would have known. Eyes that didn't meet his or eyes that did with a shrug of shoulders. Wellington and his compatriot, Dena Callahan, had done their job well. They had done a remarkable job of selling their story.

In a voice that sounded to every person in the room perceptively weaker than it had sounded just a few minutes earlier, Henry said, "Now, if I may, I would like to ask for a short recess, possibly fifteen minutes."

"There will be a fifteen minute recess," said Washington. A few walked toward the cookies at the bar, others just wanted coffee. Most took little notice of Henry's movements, but Nancy saw him walk toward his office and observed him as he closed the door behind.

CHAPTER 55

It was nearly 6 o'clock, the meeting was over two hours old, and no one in David's office had moved in all that time. They were afraid to leave fearing they would miss news from the Board Room. Then, abruptly, the phone rang. There was a momentary silence and a collectively held breath. David, who had been across the room chatting with his secretary and Lisa, seemed to bound to his desk. Before the receiver was halfway to his ear, he blurted out, "Yes?" He listened intently without any obvious expression. "Okay, get back to me when you can." He listened again and whispered a barely heard, "Thanks."

Corey Topping walked into David's office at just that moment. Now the assembled people didn't know where to look first for information. "You just finish up there?" someone asked.

"No, I was finished about forty-five minutes ago; I'm not certain what's going on right now but I can say that things weren't looking too great. Of course, that's less from what I saw and heard and more from intuition."

"Well, that was Nancy," David went on. "They've taken a break. She couldn't say much, too many people around her, she did say Henry asked for the recess and is in his office at the moment." Again, a faceless voice asked what that might mean, and Corey responded, "I wouldn't read too much into it one way or another. My gut is that Washington and Callahan did a strong job of pre-selling the board on their strategy. Having gotten that picture, Henry probably just needed some time to regroup."

"Does your gut give you any odds?" asked Mike.

Quietly, almost in a whisper, Corey said, "Not very good." He then left David's office, and David followed him into the corridor and put a hand on his shoulder.

"Corey, I know you came off great. Whatever happens, remember that you started with a major handicap; you had no board recognition. Maybe the biggest handicap of all was Mike and me having to politick with those guys. It's not a different league exactly, just a very different outlooks on things. We tried; you tried; that's all that Henry asked of us."

Corey smiled wanly and shook David's hand. He didn't say anything and headed back toward his office. David looked after him briefly and returned to his office which was still filled with a quiet group of loyal followers. It wasn't a pretty sight, he thought. Mike slid next to David and asked, "Did Corey shed light on anything that's going on up there?"

"Mike, the feeling I got was that it's a bloodbath."

CHAPTER 56

Sitting in his lounge once more, in that narrow strip of a room between the Board Room and his office, Henry stretched his tired body out on his Eckerness recliner. Back in the years before his back surgery, this chair, and one just like it at home in his bedroom, were his only source of comfort. The chair helped to ease the pain as he sat in it and leaned back. Now, no longer as afflicted by back pain since his surgery, he still found comfort sitting in it. He shut his eyes. He had removed his suit jacket and his shoes. His arms were at his side until his right arm and hand reached up into his suit jacket which he had placed on the back of a chair. He could reach to the inside pocket of the coat almost without moving of the rest of his body. This was good; his whole body was aching and very weary. From inside the pocket he pulled out the envelope and placed it on his chest, arm returning to his side. Henry breathed deeply, eyes still shut.

In his mind's eye he could see each of the faces, seven of them. Later, David would nickname them the Magnificent Seven, but at the moment they were seven men whose fate Henry held in his hands. Each of the seven had been contacted by Mike Spellari. Later, they all had conferred by phone with David. The problem had been explained to them. If they wanted to keep their company intact they had to know it was under attack, but there was a plan and they could help. The plan had been suggested by, of all people, Ruth Rothblatt, and Henry didn't know of the plan until this very morning, but David and Mike thought it had a good chance to succeed if all else was failing. As Henry sat there, he had an amused smile on his face; all else was failing he thought. The plan was simple but bold. As with most bold, crisis-solving plans, there would be risk. Controlled risk was agreeable in some cases, but in this case, if only the risk were his, he thought. Seven field managers, general agents, which included Mike, would tender their simultaneous resignations, if necessary, to keep their company from falling into the hands of Richard Washington.

These men had made promises to their clients. One of the promises was that their clients would participate as an owner in the direction of their company and in its finances. Through dividends they would be rewarded. Henry ran the phrase over and over in his mind, again and again…promise to pay.

If Henry offered up their resignations, he was reasonably certain the board would back down, but could he risk all their fates? He remembered that one of Washington's alternatives was to reduce new sales to just enough to replace policies lapsed or collected upon. A company could reduce its expenses that way and make one hell of a profit for quite awhile. He was certain, however, that was not what Washington wanted. Dick, he felt, wanted the power of running a major financial institution. Dick Washington, Henry thought, a pervert at the helm. He wouldn't use the information from the private investigators given to him months earlier by Mike and David, but he knew about it. Did he dare risk the fates of seven brave men to prevent the perverted Washington from taking control of their company?

Henry looked at the names and the signatures on the letter. He tried very hard to be a leader. People worked for leaders, he thought, but this kind of loyalty was overwhelming to him. He closed his eyes and thought back to all the wonderful moments, situations, places, and times he and Ruth had shared with these men and their families. His next thought was about how exhausted he felt. No pain. Funny, he thought. Several weeks earlier doctors had told him that their best guess was that he had about three to four months. They also told him the pain could, and probably would, get much worse. They advised him that the dreaded disease had metastasized and spread so the pain could come from almost any place in his body. He hadn't been taking any of the pain medication so he could keep his thinking clear; yet no real pain. It occurred to him that he was being provided with a window with which he could finish his business. What business? Oh God, his mind was working overtime and, while not in pain, the ever-present fatigue was taking its toll. What business? Why the business of … a twilight sleep now …. then a sound, insistent but delicate. He could not at first make it out, then he realized it was someone knocking at the door between the lounge and the Board Room. "Yes, " he called out, and the door opened a crack. It was Nancy, dear

Nancy. Did he say that out loud? No, he could not have. What he did say to her was, "Five minutes, Nancy, give me five minutes." The door shut softly.

Henry collected himself. He still needed to make a decision. Risk the careers of the seven men who had unselfishly given him their support? Jeopardize the employees, all the policyholders by allowing Washington to have his way with ICA? Mike and David had given him ammunition with which he could reasonably expect to win this war. David was such a rascal. He had the chutzpah to call six of his leading general agents and not just ask for their help; he asked them to put their careers and businesses on the line.

He knew Ruth had suggested the ploy to David after Lisa had said something about loyalty at their dinner, but David had the courage to make the calls. Mike, of course, was the seventh general agent and, Henry thought, probably the ringleader of this wonderful group of men. No, make that a wonderful group of dear friends, he mused.

As Henry bent to put on his shoes, his back suddenly stiffened. He sat up straight and stood; the lightheadedness was gone. The fatigue had relented. He pulled on his suit coat and walked into his small washroom slapping cold water on his face. He looked into the mirror and spoke out loud to himself. "Old man, David always said you were an actuary by education and profession, but the best damn salesman he had ever known. Well, Henry, you need to go back into that Board Room and make the sale of your life."

CHAPTER 57

They gathered once again. Dena and Richard sat next to each other this time. There was a subdued texture and tone to the mood of the room. They all took their seats, Nancy was poised with pen and notebook in hand. She laid both down on the table and stood, walking to the anteroom door where she once more rapped softly. This time the door opened after only one knock and she looked into the craggy face of Henry Rothblatt. He smiled at her and she was instantly energized, as he appeared to be. As he walked by her to his place she whispered quickly and quietly to him, "Give 'em hell, boss." Kind of what I have in mind, he said to himself. Did he say that to himself? I didn't say that out loud? No. He sat and looked icily at Washington. "Let's get on with it."

Richard was slightly taken aback by the remark. It made him look up, and when he did, he saw a smiling Henry. That's okay, Richard thought, but why in the hell does he look so confident? I don't think I like that look. When he left the room he was beaten. How come he didn't look beaten right now? Richard and Dena exchanged glances; Richard couldn't read her look. Does she sense something going on too? It had to be his imagination; let's just get on with it. "Gentlemen and ladies, I believe it's time for a vote on the matter of deciding on our new president. The two candidates are ..."

"Just a moment, Richard, I have something to say first."

Somewhat exasperated, "Certainly, Henry," said a now frustrated Washington. "The floor is all yours." Looking at his watch which now read 6:45 he added, "I have some reservations at 8:00; I hope we'll be finished by then." There was no laughter or response at all to his caustic remark. Barry Hornsfelt said, "We're all ears, Henry."

"Thank you, all of you. This won't take too long, though the issue is certainly important enough that time is of no concern to me." Realizing how that might sound he added, "at least not in terms of this meeting." The remark's possible other meaning was not lost on any of those present. Nancy immediately teared up.

Henry said, "I asked for a recess so I could think; I have much to consider. This company is my life. I know that's not a surprise to anyone here; obviously my feelings are that if Richard Washington leads you to vote him into the presidency of ICA, my company will be lost. Lost to me, yes, but, also lost to our employees and our policyholders. I cannot let that happen." Looking now, directly into Washington's eyes, "I will *not* let that happen."

"Richard, I do not hold anyone on this board, other than you and Ms. Callahan, responsible for the situation at hand. I'm disappointed in a few of you," he turned and faced the entire group. "After all these years how could you not believe me and listen to my appointed representatives when we tell you of the disaster Richard Washington's opportunistic ideas will bring to bear? The taking of ICA to the public marketplace will put an end to a wonderful and unusual relationship between our company and its constituencies. Employees and policyholders alike will be robbed of the culture and relationship between ICA and themselves. There's that word you so dislike, Richard, culture. A culture of trust and doing what is right."

Washington sat stoically. He was hearing a rehash, nothing new, nothing that would change anything. But then why did Henry sound so confident and strong, as if warming to his task, and why did he, Washington, feel so uncomfortable?

"I cannot let this happen, my dilemma is how to stop it. I have the bomb, but do I want to drop it? Should I drop it? The answer to these questions came to me as I sat in my office and reviewed the many years I've spent with so many wonderful people within and out of ICA. A lot of problems have been solved in my little room, and so was this one."

"Damn it, Henry, I'm certain we're all anxious to hear about whatever you have on your mind, but get on with it, please. What is it?"

"A solution, Richard."

"Yes, a solution, but get on with it, won't you?"

Richard and Dena were both aware that other board members were apparently mesmerized at the moment by Henry. One of the reasons Richard had interrupted was to break the roll, not unlike a trial lawyer objecting over nothing. The idea is to interrupt the flow. Washington grew more concerned seeing the board paying rapt attention to Henry and yet he really hadn't said much…then, Richard thought, yet. Still both Richard and Dena felt confident their majority would hold and this would all soon be over. Confident, but leery, too.

"My solution," Henry paused, "my solution consists of making certain that each member of this board fully understands the consequences of any actions the board may take. I …."

"Don't you really think this board has heard enough about what will happen if we don't elect this young squirt you're proposing? I think this board knows full well what will happen to this company…"

"Oh, you misunderstand, Richard. I'm not talking about consequences to the company or its employees or even the policyholders. I'm talking about the consequences to each of you. Consequences that will befall you as a board but also individually."

Richard, who was still standing, looked at Henry with a puzzled expression. Bob Wellington began to sense the direction here and a sly grin appeared on his face. So, he was going to drop the bomb. Bravo, Henry, bravo! Most of the board members appeared somewhat confused.

Fred Wileman stood and spoke to Washington. "Richard, may I suggest you allow Henry to explain and perhaps you could do so without interruption."

Richard sat and a bead of perspiration appeared around his lips. Dena was clearly lost in whatever was going on. It wasn't supposed to happen this way. Richard again reminded himself that, as yet, Henry had said nothing concrete or notable.

"Thank you, Fred. The consequences for each of you are these: First, you have the knowledge that the appointment of Mr. Washington would constitute the appointment of an individual with limited, very limited, experience operating a company within our industry. Furthermore, Mr. Washington has had talks, meetings, and conversations with many of you in which he disclosed the possibility of taking ICA public. Those conversations also included a description of how each of you might personally benefit from such an event. You have been advised by ICA's executive committee that neither the appointment of an inexperienced person nor the demutalization of ICA is in the interest of its present owners, our policyholders. Our executive committee and I would lead a lawsuit against all of you and each of you. At the very least, that lawsuit would substantially delay any action you could take. Richard, you have heard the term, lame duck. This company would be just such a lame duck and so, of course, would you.

"Second, our employees are none too thrilled about what's been going on around here since you were appointed vice-chair and interim president. There has been talk of a suit over a wide range of issues against you personally. I've told these employees that I and other senior officers would back them in their attempt to block your takeover."

Now, unable to contain himself, Richard Washington erupted in uncontrollable rage. "Who in the hell do you think you're bluffing here, mister? You're not talking to one of your lackeys who does your bidding without question and shakes and quivers when you enter a room. You and yours are suing no one; your precious policyholders are like sheep. One good 'boo' and they'll be running and bumping into one another. And your employees jeopardizing their pay checks is an even bigger joke. And, as for you leading the band..." Washington slowed down now. His tone and demeanor changed, turning on the proverbial dime. He had realized he was treading on dangerous ground. He realized Henry had friends even among those ready to cast their lot with him and Dena. Quietly now, "Well, Henry, I just don't think so."

"It is truly amazing to me that this company has achieved so much with so little." Henry was being sarcastic as he took up the attack again. "At least that is what you would have us believe, Mr. Washington. And how did we ever get along without your insightful leadership? We are all aware how you have accomplished so much and are so well respected within the insurance industry. Richard, why don't you dazzle us with exactly what your qualifications and accomplishments are? Why don't you tell this board what strengths you bring to the table? Maybe, I for one, will then better understand, as they say, where you're coming from. Perhaps if the executive board understood your qualifications, they could recommend you to this board; as it is, they have warned this board against your leadership."

"This board full well recognizes Richard's qualifications." A new voice, Dena Callahan, spoke up. "His leadership of Batem Electronics was exemplary. His handling of this company has been the same in the brief time he's had."

Henry interrupted. "Just a moment, Ms. Callahan. Would you suggest that ICA holding off paying legitimate claims, so that we could benefit from the earnings on holding that money, is an example of exemplary leadership?"

"We would only be doing what every other company does," Richard interrupted.

"How would you know that, did you do a study?" Henry started to continue when once more Richard exploded.

"This is crazy! Obviously Henry is talking through his hat, he has neither policyholders or employees organized. This is all just empty rhetoric in an attempt to scare this board. He wants to continue the outdated, outmoded, and stupid way ICA is being run. I suggest we get on with this vote. Henry Rothblatt is presently incapable of organizing anything or anyone."

An embarrassed silence followed. Even those who sided or agreed with Dick Washington were uncomfortable. More than one of them silently thought that whatever their feelings on the matter at hand, they were totally opposed to denigrating Henry Rothblatt in anyway whatsoever. Quickly, Washington sensed this mood and tried to turn on the charm. "People, I apologize, Henry, in the heat of debate I can get carried away. Certainly, you know how we all really feel about you."

"Yes, Dick, I think I do. By the way, would you be kind enough to read this for me, out loud if you would?" He handed an envelope to the large man who accepted it graciously and with a smile.

"Certainly, what is this exactly, Henry?"

"Just read it, if you would, please."

Richard Washington opened the envelope and as he slid out its contents, he glanced alarmingly at Dena. She, he quickly realized, had no clue either. He glanced down and began to read to the board the contents of the letter he had just removed from the envelope.

The Insurance Company of America
Board of Directors
Attn: Chairman of the Board, Henry Rothblatt

Dear Henry:

Our collective attention has been brought to the fact that Mr. Richard Washington, your appointed interim vice chairman of the board during your recovery from your recent illness, is attempting to convince board members that it would be wise to take Insurance Company of America public through the demutalization process. As you well know, the undersigned all have invested our time and considerable expense building sales organizations primarily in partnership with ICA. Much of our mutual success has been predicated on the concept of mutuality and we, and our associates, have made promises to our client policyholders. These promises included, but are not limited to, the opportunity for reduced future cost through the declaration of dividends and certain policy benefits and improvements which would keep old policies modern. These items are not usually associated with stock life insurance companies and demutalization would, we feel, rob present clients of their right to the benefits of past promises made by each of us and by ICA.

We are aware of offers being made to policyholders of other companies who have gone through the demutalization process. These offers include "buying" their interest. Our policyholders, based on our advice, have no interest in such a plan. Furthermore, Henry, we would appreciate your delivering this letter to the board as our official collective resignation should they decide to actually consummate such a plan.

Kindly remind the board that the seven undersigned individuals own agencies that control over 60 percent of ICA's in force business. Additionally, please advise the board that we will be instrumental in advising our clients of their rights and will lead a class action suit against the company, the board, and each board member.

While we cannot expect to have a direct hand in the naming of ICA's next president, we hope the board, in its wisdom, will listen closely to both our and your advice. No one knows our industry and our company as you do, and our position is that the board must recognize that a CEO, president, or chairman of ICA with little or no experience in our industry could lead to devastating consequences.

We sincerely hope the ICA board of directors will take this letter in the spirit in which it is intended. Like you, Henry, and we would hope the rest of the members of the board, we love this company and all it has stood for. We are addicted to its culture and past leadership. We hope for ourselves, our clients, and our company that the future will meld seamlessly with the past.

Sincerely,

David Camins	–	*Detroit, MI*
Richard O'Brien	–	*Los Angeles, CA*
Norton Ryan	–	*St. Paul, MN*
Lee Zorn	–	*Cleveland, OH*
Robert Frisch	–	*San Francisco, CA*
Benjamin Galter	–	*Atlanta, GA*
Michael Spellari	–	*Chicago, IL*

As Richard finished reading the letter there was stone cold silence in the room. All of them realized the tide had changed. ICA could not risk intrusion upon or loss of 60 percent of its business, not to mention the fact that others might very well follow the lead of these seven men. It was slowly sinking in, and they began exchanging words with those around them. It was as though several coffee klatches were going on at the same time.

Abruptly, Washington stood, his chair was knocked backwards and almost over. His face was crimson with rage. It looked as if the blood of his body had drained upward from his feet to his head and all of it was accumulating in his cheeks, nose, and forehead. "This is all utterly stupid," he bellowed. "Do any of you actually take this so-called resignation letter seriously? Do you really think that these men would jeopardize their own businesses? It's a bluff. They just want something for themselves out of whatever actions we take. Well, why not. There will be plenty for everyone, anyway. We'll give them a piece of the action, stock options or whatever."

Dena sat without moving. She had barely heard anything Richard had just said. That sly old fox, she thought. What a trump card he had just played. She couldn't help but think how exciting it might have been to be a part of Henry's life when he was younger and healthier, but no, she had to pick out the Richard Washingtons, pompous, power-hungry idiots who would fold at the first sign of trouble. She didn't even bother to wonder if there were any way to save the situation. She knew it was far too late for that.

Barry Hornsfelt now took the floor. "Richard, I personally know at least three of those seven men, and I can tell you they are dead serious. If they say they will resign, they will resign. Count on it."

"And I know them all." Bob Wellington rose from his place. Somehow he looked taller and leaner than he had when he entered the room. "Barry is exactly right, they will do whatever they say they will. They will do exactly what they say, lawsuits and all."

Bob now turned his attention to Richard. "The problem you have, old man, is a complete inability to understand that the culture you so despise is exactly the thread that ties the loyalty of these men to Henry and ICA. Their loyalty to their clients is part of the same culture. These men are fearless entrepreneurs; they're not afraid to start over if necessary. And neither your pomposity nor your rage will scare them one bit."

Barry then said, "I would like to call for a vote on the issue of the presidency of ICA." Now he looked directly at Henry. "Mr. Chairman," he said loudly in a strong voice, "will you please call the vote?"

Henry returned the look and spoke clearly and with assurance. "Yes, yes, I will."

Within ten minutes the vote had been taken and Corey Topping had been elected as the new president and probably future chairman of the board of ICA.

Wellington, after announcing the results, spoke to the group as a whole, though clearly all present knew to whom his remarks were directed. "As you all know, our bylaws require that a director hold an appropriate title in his full time position. If a director should lose that title, for any reason, he or she has eighteen months to assume a new position with similar title, otherwise they may no longer hold a position on this board. Mr. Washington has been previously advised of this rule both by me and by Mr. Hornsfelt.

"Mr. Washington, you have until the last day of this month to fulfill that obligation; otherwise your services to this board, as of December 31, will terminate. Of course you may always choose to resign before then."

Shell-shock might be the best way to describe Richard's condition at that moment. He barely heard what Bob Wellington was saying. He only too clearly understood his situation. He said nothing. It was his final time in the ICA Board Room, and he never did resign.

CHAPTER 58

Henry returned to his office after having accepted the congratulations of the board. Of course that did not include Richard Washington or Dena Callahan. Barry and Bob had embraced him in joy. He was weary, that was certain, but he had called for Mike and David along with Corey to meet in his office. He wanted to congratulate Corey and set up a schedule for them to meet and begin the transition. Henry would somehow muster his strength to stand and embrace Michael and David, and he would also ask them to arrange a victory celebration. A party to include the executive committee, Nancy, and most certainly the "Magnificent Seven"; bring them to Chicago with their wives and party.

Somehow he'd find the strength but it would have to happen very soon.

CHAPTER 59

Richard Washington had not been seen or heard from for several days. No one knew where he was, much less what he was doing, and no one seemed to care. David and Lisa had not seen each other since the day of the board meeting. Lisa had an overseas trip. She would make it back on the afternoon of the great celebration. Mike and David had jointly put a party hastily together. They consulted with Henry who insisted the "Magnificent Seven" and their wives be included in any plans. Nancy, of course, also received her invitation. Additionally, the entire executive committee along with a few others would all be there. No board members other than Bob and Barry Hornsfelt were invited. It was a political decision. Henry felt the party should be primarily for those who helped to save the day.

On a Friday night, exactly two weeks after the board had elected Corey Topping, he hosted a celebration party in honor of the company's victory "over the forces of evil," as the joke went. Most everyone was in a joyful spirit. The holidays and the victory combined were providing a smiling, laughing crowd in Gibsons upstairs private room. Barring a last minute change in his condition, why not steak for Henry who had never met a piece of meat he didn't like?

The room was set up with a bar and two bartenders in one corner, along with eight tables set for ten people each. At 6:30 the crowd at the private bar munched on hors d'oeuvres. They sipped their drinks and they could talk of little else but speculate on what condition Henry would arrive in. His health was a constant topic of conversation, and few had seen him since the day of the board meeting.

Laughing over one of David's best jokes, Mike Spellari couldn't help noticing how beautiful Lisa looked. He was happy for David, who made no attempt to hide his feelings. He held Lisa's hand or had his arm around her at every opportunity.

The seven courageous men who had risked so much to set up the ultimate outcome gathered together in another corner having just had their pictures taken as a group, at David's request. There was much back-slapping and hand-shaking and, other than those persistent questions about Henry's health, the hot topic of conversation had to do with what Henry might say to them this evening. There was also substantial curiosity as to the whereabouts of Dick Washington.

About 7 o'clock they all heard someone announce, "They're here." The crowd edged toward the doorway and Mike and David found themselves right up at the front. Lenny, Henry's driver, entered first, then Henry followed by Ruth. She and Lenny each had one arm through each of Henry's. The laughter and mirth came to a crashing halt. Appearing before them was a man with sunken, blackened eyes, wearing a suit of clothes that looked as though it might fall off his bent, frail body. He walked, but in very short staccato steps. At first his head was bowed, but as he began to realize he was now among his people, he braced his shoulders and lifted his head. Then a thin smile appeared and, as if by magic, he lit up the room and suddenly there was life in it again. The euphoria of seeing his people momentarily energized him and Henry gently shrugged away from the arms that held him and slowly shuffled to where Mike and David stood, Lisa by David's side. When Henry pulled up in front of them, he looked at Lisa and in a small voice you would have to strain to hear, he simply said, "Hello, dear," as he reached for her hand. Lisa smiled at him, as tears streamed down her cheeks.

Henry slowly turned toward David. The two men's eyes locked. They communicated telepathically: "We did it. We saved ICA." They sent that message, among others, to each other. Henry's hand reached out and it lifted David's tie. Looking at it momentarily, Henry looked up at his protégé's face and said, "Someday, when I can afford it, I'm going to get me a tie like this." Then the two men embraced. For the first time since he had known Henry, he saw a tear in the man's eye and that caused David to grab Henry's neck, pulling it gently to him and whispering, "You can have it anytime you want it." They stood, momentarily locked in an embrace, until Henry let him know he needed to sit.

By the time a salad was served Henry had been discretely taken from the room and returned home. He said nothing publicly at the party, or ever again. He was seen only once more by Bob Wellington, David, Corey and Mike. Four days after the party, Henry Rothblatt, the indestructible Henry Rothblatt, passed away peacefully in his sleep. Ruth was with him, as were his children.

Henry Rothblatt, President and Chairman of the Board of ICA for the past twenty years had died said the <u>Tribune</u>'s obituary. It should have said so much more.

CHAPTER 60

They came from around the country to pay their final respects to this corporate patriarch, to this beloved man who had influenced so many lives. He had passed on like the gentle person he was, having asked for no heroic measures.

At the cemetery, after the service, Ruth approached Mike and David and asked if they would be coming back to the house for the traditional shiva. This was the Jews version of a wake. A party for the living, designed to celebrate the deceased.

"Of course," said David.

"Good, I want to show you both something," Ruth had replied. Neither David nor Mike thought much about it, but they were curious.

The house, which Henry had so loved, was crowded with friends of the family, relatives, and business associates. About 7 o'clock that evening, David, who had driven both Mike and Lisa, suggested that if they left, maybe others would follow, and Ruth could get a much needed night's sleep. When they started gathering their coats, Ruth caught sight of them from the corner of her eye. She walked toward them. "Just a minute. Remember, I have something to show you both." She had reached them and took each of their hands. "Come with me." After nodding her head at Lisa, to let her know she was included, she turned and walked with the three of them at her heels. In a few seconds they found themselves in Ruth and Henry's bedroom. Ruth walked to the night stand on Henry's side of the bed. They followed her and watched as she picked up one of two picture frames that stood on the stand. The first photograph was of Ruth and Henry when they were in perhaps their forties in front of a lake somewhere; the second, which Ruth now held in her hand, she handed to David. Lisa and Mike slid close to his side to get a look.

It was a snapshot of Henry, Mike, and David all holding golf clubs. David instantly recognized it as being from an ICA convention in Palm Springs about two years earlier.

"He kept this at his bedside for the past couple of years because waking up and looking at it made him smile. It got his day off to a good start." Ruth softly choked back her emotion. "He loved you both so much."

She reached for their hands and they slowly backed away as Lisa looked at David. Once more tears rolled down both of their cheeks, as they did from Mike's. Lisa gently put her hand on David's shoulder and David put his arm around Mike's shoulder. They stood closely together and wept. After a few moments David said, "You know, he never paid me for the last time I beat him. Damn it, Henry, hell of a way to avoid a debt." Ruth and Mike smiled, Lisa smiled, David grasped the picture to his chest, then set it back gently on the night stand, and he too smiled.

PROMISE TO PAY

BY
ROBERT S. LEVITZ

Available at your local bookstore or use this page to order.

--1-931633-91-6- Promise to Pay - $15.50 U.S
Send to: Trident Media Inc.
801 N. Pitt Street #123
Alexandria, VA 22314
Toll Free # 1-877-874-6334
Please send me the item above. I am enclosing
$_____(please add $4.50 per book to cover postage and handling).
Send check, money order, or credit card:

Card #_____ Exp. date _____

Mr./Mrs./Ms._____
Address_____
City/State_____Zip_____

Please allow four to six weeks for delivery.
Prices and availability subject to change without notice.

Printed in the United States
1254400001B/205-210